The Moment She Was Gone

A Novel

EVAN HUNTER

SIMON & SCHUSTER
New York London Toronto Sydney Singapore

SIMON & SCHUSTER
Rockefeller Center
1230 Avenue of the Americas
New York, NY 10020

SIMON & SCHUSTER and colophon are registered trademarks
of Simon & Schuster, Inc.

Designed by Lauren Simonetti

Manufactured in the United States of America

ISBN 0-7432-3748-X

This is for my beloved wife,
Dragica Dimitrijević-Hunter,
who nursed it along patiently and
devotedly—and finally blessed it.
My eternal thanks and enduring love.

The Moment She Was Gone

1

My mother phones me the moment Annie is gone.

It is two o'clock in the morning.

I know at once who is calling and why. Nobody but my mother ever calls me at two in the morning, and then only to tell me that my sister is gone again.

❑

The family gathers in the early morning hours. I get there last because I live in Chelsea, all the way downtown, and my mother's apartment is on West End Avenue and Eighty-first Street. They are already talking about what to do when I come in. My sister-in-law Augusta offers me a cup of coffee, and then we go in to join the others in the living room.

My mother is sixty-three years old, but she still skis and she still travels and there are many people who find her attractive. When I look at her, I see a thin, hawkish-faced woman with piercing green eyes and short brown hair she tints auburn. She is wearing tonight a brocaded silk robe she bought in Tokyo three summers ago, and red velvet slippers with gold trim, from Bergdorf's. My mother is very proud of her tiny feet. She tells everyone she knows, over and over again, that she has truly tiny feet and then immediately informs them that she once played Alice in a touring company of *Alice in Wonderland,* as if her tiny feet had been responsible for her getting the role.

My mother was once a stage actress, you see. Helene Hammond was her stage name, does it ring a bell? I wouldn't guess so. She hasn't performed in anything since she was part of the young cast in *West Side Story*—the original Broadway production, that is—back in 1957. That was forty-five years ago. But she still thinks of herself as a musical comedy star, which she never really was.

My mother's maiden name was Helene Lederer. That's because she's Jewish. I feel certain my grandmother intended her name to be pronounced "Ell-*enn,*" in the French manner, an affectation common among well-to-do Jews of her generation. Instead, my mother pronounces it to rhyme with Arlene. I personally feel the French pronunciation would better suit her personality, but it's her name and her business. According to my older brother, our mother's Jewishness makes all of her kids Jewish as well, even though my father was an Irishman named Terrence Gulliver.

I say "was" because I never really got to know the man. He abandoned my mother and the family when I was only five years old. Well, divorced her. My mother keeps saying he abandoned her, even though he paid alimony and child support till Annie and I turned eighteen. Like me, Annie was also five when Daddy left, so you can't blame her problems on his defection. Annie is my twin, you see. Andrew and Anne, as our parents named us. Andy and Annie, as we became, no relation to the Raggedys.

My brother is quite successful. His name is Aaron, which was my mother's father's name. My grandfather turned all of Mama's pictures to the wall the moment he learned she was going to marry a starving artist named Terrence Gulliver. By the time my father jumped ship, he was no longer a starving artist, and my hypocritical Hungarian grandfather was calling him "Terry, m'lad," according to bitter stories my mother still tells, but it turned out the old man was right after all, wasn't he? Not wanting her to marry a goy?

My grandfather is now dead, but his namesake—my brother Aaron—is the CEO of a cosmetics firm with which you're familiar if you're any woman who tints her hair, go ask my mother. Aaron agrees he's Jewish because our mother is Jewish. That's okay by me. His daughters are not Jewish, however. That's because Aaron's wife is of German descent. In fact, his daughters aren't even his true daughters, in that . . .

Well, that's another story.

❑

You see, after Aaron brought his intended bride home to meet the family, my mother instantly hired a private detective from Newark to look into the "young lady's background."

It appeared that my brother was about to marry the town whore.

The detective reported that Augusta was knocked up for the first time in the back seat of a Chevy convertible parked behind the football stadium at Ridley High School in Ridley Hills, New Jersey. The father of her first daughter was a quarterback for the Ridley Royals, as they still call themselves, a rather pretentious name for a team that has finished at the bottom of its league from time immemorial.

Michael Henderson, for such was his name, never married Augusta—or Gussie as she was calling herself back then. Instead, he ran off to join a commune in San Francisco. Gussie somehow persuaded her staid Lutheran parents to let her go ahead with the birth rather than have the baby aborted. Augusta is now forty-five years old. Her first

3

daughter, Lauren, is twenty-nine and married. Mr. Henderson must have spread little Gussie's legs (presumably not for the first time) when she was but a mere fifteen.

When she was sixteen, and three months after Lauren was born, Augusta took on a brawny lad named Colin O'Rourke, this time on the football field itself, the better to enjoy the splendor in the grass, no doubt. Lo and behold, and having learned nothing about birth control on her earlier go-round, Augusta discovered that she was once again pregnant. Young Colin, left tackle but devout Catholic, also chose not to marry her, preferring instead to enlist in the United States Army. He was whisked almost at once to a post in peacetime Germany, where he was killed in an automobile accident on the Autobahn. Augusta's first child was only a year old when the second one was born. In honor of her slain Irish swain, she named this second daughter Kelly.

My brother Aaron was twenty-two when he met Augusta. He was a senior at Princeton, which is not far from Ridley Hills, if you have a map. She was twenty-seven, and working at the time as a counter girl at the local McDonald's. By then, gun-shy Gussie had developed a reputation for swallowing organs larger than the one at Radio City Music Hall, a talent my brother apparently found engaging as well as engorging. Gussie's daughters were eleven and ten respectively, and still bore her maiden surname, Manners, the Anglicized Mannheim from which town her forbears had migrated. Manners, no less. A singular contradiction when one considers that etiquette is the least of Augusta's attributes. By the way, she started calling herself Augusta again the moment my stupid-ass brother slipped a wedding band on her dainty trembling hand.

He has since adopted both daughters. They are now, respectively and respectfully, Lauren Gulliver Hastings and Kelly Gulliver. When my mother dies, Augusta and Aaron will undoubtedly inherit a share of her estate which—when *they* die—will go to the offspring of two-elevenths of the Ridley Royals' offensive team.

Augusta had no qualms about seeking an abortion six years ago, however, when at the age of thirty-nine she surprisingly missed two periods in a row, and quick as a wink deduced, Gee, I must be preggers again, wow. This was a woman, mind you, who—when I suggested that she vote for a freedom-of-choice candidate because one day either one of her two lovely daughters might find herself in trouble and in desperate need of an abortion—said, "Oh, *that!*" and airily waved aside the entire anti-abortion issue. It wasn't a matter of "Oh, *that!*" some four years later, however, when a doctor confirmed that she was indeed pregnant, and Augusta decided she was too old to be bearing another child, they're either too young or too old, right? Quicker than you could say "Right to Life," Augusta found a respectable doctor who aborted the embryos.

You heard me correctly.

Embryos.

Plural.

Two of them.

Augusta had been bearing twins.

I have never forgiven Aaron for that.

I felt he and his wife had flushed my own heritage down the drain.

❑

Annie believes she is an adept who has been initiated into a form of Tantric yoga.

Her tongue is pierced. She wears a little silver circlet in it, which she says she purchased at a bazaar in Katmandu. She wears another silver circlet through her left nostril (Hong Kong) and yet another through the brow over her right eye (Sri Lanka). Kissing Annie hello is like kissing a jewelry tray. She also has a tattoo on her right buttock, a swastika above the words *Ek Xib Chac* in red, below which are the words *Chac Xib Chac* in black, which she says translates as "The red and the black," though she did not mention in which language, probably Sanskrit. She says she acquired the tattoo in Berlin before the wall came down, and before she headed for more exotic places. She proudly explained to a dining room full of dinner guests on one of her frequent stays in my mother's apartment that the swastika was an ancient and treasured symbol in her religion, and might have exhibited her tattoo if my mother hadn't called everyone to coffee and dessert in the living room just then.

Annie tells me she once ate sweet potatoes and later shat in the woods with native tribesmen in Papua New Guinea. She tells me she was mauled by a tiger in a remote section of India, the name of which I can't even pronounce, but which falls ever so trippingly off my sister's tongue.

I no longer know if any of these things are real or merely figments of Annie's fertile imagination.

Ever since what happened in Sicily a month and a half ago, I simply do not know.

❏

Whenever Annie runs away, I blame my mother.

I blame her because she keeps giving Annie money even though she's been advised time and again that she is just pissing the money down the toilet. My sister-in-law Augusta doesn't like my mother to give Annie money, either, but that's because she's fearful her two daughters won't inherit as much when Grandma dies. In that respect, Annie and she are soulmates. My sister often talks about friends of hers who have inherited huge sums of money, or luxurious houses, or acres and acres of undeveloped land in Florida. She seems to think my mother is enormously wealthy. I don't know what gives her this idea; there is no empirical evidence to support such a notion of wealth. My mother's apartment on West End looks like the shabby abode of a European lady who has seen better times. The furniture is shoddy, the drapes need cleaning. There is the faint odor of mustiness and age clinging to everything. And yet, she keeps sending money to Annie.

I think she's afraid my sister will become a prostitute or a homeless person. I think she's afraid she will be blamed for my sister's destitute state, if it ever comes to that. Even before Sicily we were all a little afraid of that. Afraid we'd be held responsible somehow if anything happened to her. Jewish guilt. My brother may be right. We may all of us be Jews, after all. Except my sister-in-law and her two bastard children.

So here we are on a hot muggy night in August, commiserating and plotting because Annie has fled once again, and we're all afraid that before morning Sicily will happen all over again.

❑

Then again, Annie has always run away, with or without seeming provocation. In fact, she has been traveling all over the world without incident ever since—

Well, that isn't quite true.

On the other hand, it's *almost* true.

Except for that one crazy week in Italy a month and a half ago, Annie has managed to keep out of serious trouble for most of her life. Sicily was the only episode . . . well, incident . . . well, episode . . . I promise you, the only one.

The family has heard various versions of what happened, most of them from Annie herself, one of them from yours truly who went to Italy to "rescue" her, as Annie puts it. After everything Bertuzzi told me, I don't know which parts of her story are true. It's a known fact, of course, that there are banditos on the road in various isolated parts of Italy, and especially in Sicily where my sister had gone to seek out the wisdom of a guru whose name I still can't pronounce and whose presence in Italy, of all places, I still sincerely doubt. But possibly the bandito part of her story is true, no matter what Bertuzzi says.

Before the incident—well, episode—Annie told us she was living in a room she rented from the village butcher. This was undoubtedly true. She told us she had met a German girl from Frankfurt, possibly also true, who like herself was an initiate, and who—again like herself— was in Sicily to seek further enlightenment and inspiration from Abu Ben Pipik or whatever his name was.

According to Annie, she and Lise were enjoying a bottle of cheap Sicilian red at a quiet outdoor table under a grape arbor when two Italian "roughs," as Annie later called them, approached the table and began making fun of her rings, the one in her nose, yes, and the one over her eye, but especially the one in her tongue.

I have to tell you that my sister generally takes exceptionally good care of herself. She is three inches shorter than I am, which makes her five-nine, and she weighs a hundred and thirty pounds, which makes her slender—well, before she went to Italy, she'd let herself go a bit, but I would guess by the time of the trouble there, she was back in good shape again. When Annie isn't sitting silent and motionless in the lotus position, practicing yoga, she is doing sit-ups or pushups or jogging in place. She is extremely fit. We both have green eyes—Aaron's are blue, but thank you, anyway, Mom. We both have blond hair—so does Aaron, thank you unconditionally, Terrence Gulliver, wherever you may be. Annie's hair is blonder than mine, almost flaxen, in fact, but that's because on her travels ("Gulliver's Travels," we sometimes call them) she spends a great deal of time in the sun. Altogether, my sister looks like what the guys on the singles scene in New York might call a babe. So it is understandable that a pair of Sicilian youths on the prowl might have approached the table where she and Lise were in deep conversation. That part of the story is possibly true, though Bertuzzi thinks it's all imagined.

Annie isn't fluent in any language except English, but she does have a smattering of French and Italian, so maybe her recounting of the dialogue at the table is accurate. In any case, in yet *another* retelling of the story, Lise was fluent in Italian, including the Neapolitan *and* Sicilian dialects, and it was she who was doing the translating. Here, then, is how the conversation at the table went, as translated by a German girl from Frankfurt, repeated later by Annie, and sincerely doubted by Bertuzzi.

"Hey, girls, you want some company?"

"No, thank you, we're having a little private talk here."

This from my sister.

"But thank you for asking."

This from Lise; my sister insists it encouraged a further dialogue.

"Why are you wearing a ring over your eye?"

"None of your business."

"How about the one in your nose?"

"Ditto."

"Doesn't it get in the way when you kiss?"

"Boys, we're not interested, okay?"

"Are you lesbians?"

This may seem like far too sophisticated a comment from an ignorant Sicilian farmer, but remember that if a woman isn't interested in an Italian man's obvious charms, she *must* be queer. On the other hand, I myself have often wondered about Annie's sexual orientation, so it's entirely possible that she and Lise were enjoying more than just a private conversation at their hidden table. In one of Annie's tellings, they were meditating. In another, they were holding hands. In a third version, they were holding hands *and* meditating. Given the question about the nose ring getting in the way of kissing, might they not have been kissing as well? Who knows? I sometimes think my sister wrote the screenplay for *Rashomon*.

It was the next few questions that started the fracas.

"Why do you have a ring in your tongue?"

"Doesn't it get in the way when you lick your friend's pussy?"

Oops.

Annie grabbed the bottle of red by its neck.

Like the good second baseman and power hitter she once used to be when she and I were young and happy together in summers gone by, she swung the bottle at the head of the lout who'd made the remark, hitting him over the left eye. The bottle broke, spilling red wine all over his white shirt, and opening a gash some four inches long in his bushy eyebrow. Soaking wet and gushing blood, he began cursing in the dialect, seemingly more concerned about his wine-stained shirt than the wound over his eye. His pal went pale. So did Lise the Brave, who immediately raced off into the night. Annie got up, knocking over her chair, and swinging the jagged edge of the bottle in a wide circle as she backed off the terrace and down the steps and out of the place.

That isn't the end of the story.

As the tale unfolds . . .

She throws the broken bottle into the scraggly bushes lining the dusty road, and thinks at first she should go back to her tiny room over the butcher shop, but wouldn't those roughs in the bar know where she lives? Or wouldn't they ask the proprietor of the bar where she lives, everyone *knows* she lives right over the butcher shop! So she heads up the mountain instead. It is close to midnight on a Friday night on a lonely Sicilian road. My sister has no specific plan in mind except *not* to go back to the dubious safety of her room over the butcher shop. At first, she's not sure she's actually seeing figures in the road ahead of her. She stops, peers into the darkness.

There are four men in the road ahead. Four men blocking the road that leads up the mountain and to safety, if we are to understand her reasoning. The leader of the four—the one she assumes is the leader—says something to her in Italian, in the Sicilian dialect, no less, which of course she can't understand. Instead of picking up her skirts—she is wearing a peasant blouse and a wide peasant skirt and sandals she bought in a shop in Palermo before beginning her inland trek—instead of picking up her skirts and running *down* the mountain and away from the imminent threat posed by these four hulking men blocking the road ahead of her, their manner and their unintelligible speech promising pillage and rape on a grand scale, banditos for sure, instead of running down the hill *away* from them . . . she smiles.

I happen to believe this.

I know my sister.

She would have smiled.

Besides, from time immemorial, women have smiled in the face of imminent rape. Smiling at a would-be rapist is the equivalent of smiling around a pistol someone has thrust in your mouth. Especially if you have a ring piercing your tongue. But smile she does, and then explains to them, in English, of course, that she is an American, and she wishes they would let her proceed up the mountain in peace. The only word they understand is "American." So, naturally, they pounce upon her, and pummel her, and throw her to the ground, and rape her, all four of them, one at a time, or so her story goes.

I have heard this tale and its many variations several times now.

It is the tale she initially told the police in Mistretta, and later the magistrate there, and finally Dr. Lorenzo Bertuzzi, the psychiatrist at Ospedale Santa Chiara. Maybe it's true. I still want to believe it really happened.

As the tale unfolds . . .

Her rapists leave her battered and bruised on the dusty road in the dark, laughing as they go off into the endless night. Her panties are torn, her blouse ripped open over her breasts. Her lip is bleeding. She is bruised all over, she hurts all over. She stumbles to her feet and starts *down* the mountain at last, back toward the village where perhaps the two roughs are still looking for her, but where at least there are policemen to whom she can report this outrage, at least there are telephones, at least there are civilized human beings!

But on the way down the mountain . . .

On her way back to civilization . . .

On her way back to safety . . .

She sees a light coming from a wooden shack just off the road. It is a quarter to one in the morning. The crystal on her watch is broken from when she was on her back struggling and her attackers spread her arms wide and held her hands and her wrists to the dusty road, pinning her there . . .

The broken watch crystal is real. I happen to know that for a fact. I saw the watch when I went to the hospital to pick her up. It was a cheap little watch with a plastic band. The crystal was indeed broken, but the watch was still ticking. Now whether or not the crystal got broken during a rape is another story. The doctors who initially examined

Annie at the hospital found no lacerations about the labia or tears of the vaginal wall, no signs of forced entry, no traces of sperm in the vaginal vault. In their opinion my sister was not raped that Friday night.

There is a light burning in the small shack.

She approaches the front door.

She knocks.

"*Chi è?*"

A man's voice.

She understands the Italian. He is asking who is here at his front door at a quarter to one in the morning.

"*Sono io,*" she says. And then, because she learned the word to use in case of an emergency just like this one, "*Aiuto!*"

"It's me! Help!"

The door opens.

A massive man is standing in the doorframe, lighted from behind. He is bald, totally bald, and naked to the waist, and barefooted. He is wearing only trousers fastened at the waist with a black belt.

He looks at her.

Without a word, he reaches out for her, seizes her by the arms, both arms, grabs her just above the biceps, and . . .

("It's called a head butt," Annie tells us. "Men in Europe are skilled at it. They know how to bang their heads against yours with unbelievable force and yet sustain no injury to themselves. It's a skill they have.")

He pulls her toward him, his head moving forward at the same time. Their heads collide. She stumbles away from him, dizzied by the blow, staggers across the road, loses her footing, falls to her knees, rolls over—and suddenly she is falling down the mountain! Tumbling and rolling and bouncing and jostling, she finally comes to a stop on yet another dusty road below, and lies motionless and breathless on her back under the stars. She does not move for ten minutes, fifteen, perhaps longer. Then she stumbles to her feet and begins walking again, not back to the village where all of this started, but instead to the nearest real town, Mistretta, where there is a proper constabulary that will take note and make record of the various indignities she has suffered this night.

She tells the police she was accosted by two roughs in the bar in town, and then assaulted and raped by four banditos on the road up the mountain, and then head-butted by a brute of a man who lives in a shack on the side of the mountain, after which dizzying blow, she fell down the mountain. She shows them her bruises, her cuts, her bumps and lumps. She tells them she wants them to go up the mountain to arrest the brute who butted her with his knobby bald head, and then find the banditos who assaulted and raped her, and then go over to the village to arrest the roughs in the bar who started all this. She tells them her father is a famous painter. She tells them he is Terrence Gulliver. She does not tell them that she hasn't seen him since she was five years old. Standing disheveled and wild-eyed in a police station at two in the morning, she tells the police she wants them to arrest half the male populace of Sicily. The police cluck their tongues and shake their heads in sympathy, *Ah, questi Americani!* But they are not about to go out into the night in search of men they already suspect are phantoms. Finally, in desperation, my sister tells them she will kill herself if they don't protect her somehow.

The cops tossed Annie into a cell, and locked the door, and kept her there until nine the next morning, when the local magistrate came to work, at which time they informed him that they had a crazy American here who was threatening to kill herself. My sister repeated the entire story to the magistrate, who listened carefully, especially when she told him she would kill herself if he did not immediately issue an arrest warrant for the seven men who had accosted her. Instead, the magistrate had her remanded to the nearest hospital, a place named Ospedale Santa Chiara, perched on a mountaintop overlooking the verdant plains.

❑

A man named Gianfreddo Mazzoni called my mother from Naples to say that her daughter had been confined to "a mental hospital" in Sicily, and then asked at once if Annie's father was really a famous painter. Apparently, the people at Santa Chiara were used to patients claiming their fathers were Pablo Picasso, or Leonardo da Vinci, or Prince Albert, or even Jesus Christ. My mother informed Mr. Mazzoni that she and Mr. Gulliver had been divorced for thirty-one years now (but who was counting), however, yes, he *was* rather well-known in art circles. "If that's why you've put my daughter in a mental hospital . . ." she started to say, but Mazzoni informed her at once that Annie had been admitted in a violent state and had been medicated and re-strained, and did someone want to come to Italy to arrange for her re-lease and transportation home?

Annie had indeed been restrained and medicated. She reported this to me on the phone after I got past a multitude of Sicilians who could not speak English, and then a social worker whose English was faulty at best, and at last got through to Annie herself, who seemed bemused by it all and who insisted there was no need for me to travel all the way from America, she was learning a lot of Italian songs, everyone was being very nice to her, everyone liked her a lot, everyone smiled at her all the time.

On the phone, Annie told me the hospital had a small mental ward, to which she'd been transferred on her second day there, after she re-fused medication and was put in a strait jacket. That was when Mama found out she'd been hospitalized. Before then, it was all a lark to Annie. The hospital was crowded and so they put her on a wheeled bed in the corridor outside the maternity ward. She could see women com-ing in bloated with pregnancy and leaving days later with babies in their arms. The women taught her Italian songs. She could walk down the hall and look in at the newborn babies row on row, "like pink flow-ers in a garden," she told me. She felt safe here. Her little ruse had worked. "I never *intended* killing myself," she told me on the phone. "That was a trick to get away from the guys who were chasing me. I *knew* if I threatened suicide, they'd send me to a hospital." She did not tell me why they thought she'd needed medication—which, of course, she'd refused—or why, if she was so calm and serene and singing Italian songs and looking in at little pink-faced Italian babies, they'd felt compelled to move her to the mental ward, in a strait jacket, no less. But the situation must have suddenly stopped looking like *The Wizard of Oz* along about then, must have seemed threatening enough, in fact ("One of the orderlies began fondling me while I was tied to the bed"), for her to have requested a telephone call to the American Consulate in Naples.

The medication they'd given her was Risperdal.

"This is the brand name for risperidone," Bertuzzi tells me. "It is an antipsychotic agent used for the management of acute psychotic episodes and accompanying violent behavior in patients with schizophrenia."

This is the first time he has mentioned the word "schizophrenia." We are sitting in his office at the hospital, a high-ceilinged room in what once used to be a nunnery, huge windows overlooking the green hills beyond. It is a beautiful day at the end of June, but the good doctor is telling me my sister is psychotic. He sits behind a large oaken desk strewn with case folders. He sports a gray Vandyke beard that matches the color of his wrinkled linen suit. His English is accented, but impeccable. His eyes are so brown they appear black. He never smiles. I notice he never smiles. He is obviously not kidding when he tells me he knows for sure my sister is nuts.

"That is to say, she hears voices," he tells me. "Which means she's hallucinatory. And yes, she's delusional, as well, in that she believes the FBI is following her around in blue windbreakers that have the letters FBI printed on them in bright yellow."

I look at him.

But I say nothing.

"In the literature," he says, "delusions and hallucinations are called Criterion-A symptoms, and only one of them is required for a diagnosis of schizophrenia if the delusions are bizarre. Or if the hallucinations consist of a single voice keeping up a running commentary on the

15

person's behavior. Or if two or more voices are conversing with each other."

"I don't know why you think my sister is hearing . . ."

"It would be comforting to think of her as suffering from a mere delusional disorder," he says, blithely unaware that I am listening to his talk of voices in total disbelief, "rather than a serious mental illness like schizophrenia, except for the fact that two of the A criteria for schizophrenia have been met, and her delusions are not simple non-bizarre delusions like being followed, or poisoned, or infected . . ."

"Any of your everyday, garden-variety delusions," I say, but he does not smile.

"Your sister's delusions involve full scale investigations by the FBI, whose agents follow her twenty-four hours a day, seven days a week. She thinks it's because she once had a roommate who was a translator for the UN. Has she never mentioned . . . ?"

"Dr. Bertuzzi, I think you're making a terrible mistake here. I don't know what sort of medication you've been giving her . . ."

"I told you. Risperdal."

"Well, it seems to have inspired . . ."

"On the contrary, it has subdued the voices for the time being. I know it would be more comfortable to accept a less significant diagnosis like paranoid personality disorder," he says, "but the literature specifically states that paranoid personality disorder must be ruled out as a diagnosis if the pattern of behavior—persistent delusions and hallucinations—occurs exclusively during the course of schizophrenia, which is most certainly the case here."

"Thank you, Doctor, but I hope you won't mind if I ask for a second opinion, hmm?"

"Yes, I would in fact suggest you do that as soon as you get back to America. The injection we gave her should wear off relatively soon, but I'll prescribe medication that should keep your sister stable for a month or so. However, Mr. Gulliver, believe me, *è rotto*," he says, suddenly reverting to his native Italian. "Her brain, do you understand? *È rotto.* Her brain is broken."

❑

My sister has been in trouble since she was sixteen, I can't pretend she hasn't. In fact, from the first time she ran off to Europe alone, Annie has been the star of our little family show. A day does not go without our discussing Annie's whereabouts, or her well-being, or her finances. Not a single day. Annie has been the central concern in our lives for the past eternity now. Or perhaps longer.

But before Sicily, no one ever told us she was mentally ill.

So now the family gathers in the empty hours of the night, and wonders what on earth we are to do.

2

July 5, 2002

Andy: I know I promised you and Mom that I'd join you for the
big sit-down today, but something's come up, and I'm afraid I'll
have to bow out. In fact, I'll be leaving for New Orleans almost
as soon as I fire off this e-mail; a car to the airport is picking me
up at eleven. Sorry for the late notice, but this just came up late
yesterday afternoon.

I know you'll be discussing what next to do about Annie, so
let me give you my thoughts on the matter, for whatever they're
worth. Annie is entirely set in her ways. Mom told me it's okay
for her to stay there for a while, but I suspect she will take off
again before long. That is her pattern. When she runs out of
money, she'll be in touch. She's been doing that since she was sixteen. It's a basic mode, and it won't change. Meanwhile, there's
not much any of us can do, except to accept the idea that Annie

is incapable of seeing her situation or her own acts clearly. Annie listens to no one but herself. Sorry, but that's the way it is. I have too much to do right now to waste time on Annie.

The best thing she could do would be to take up residence someplace and stay there a good long while, but she is incapable of making any kind of decision right now, or accepting counsel. The best thing you can do right now is take Annie for what she is. She's never going to change, so you might as well get used to that idea. Regards, Aaron.

P.S. One thing I do want to warn you against. If you're considering putting her up here in New Jersey with Augusta and me, don't even think it.

❑

I am not surprised that Augusta is refusing to have my sister in her house. She has been doing that for as long as I've known her. In fact, Augusta abandoned this entire family the moment my brother slipped a gold band on her finger. Until then, she was Miss Mousy Tiptoes, hiding behind my brother's considerable girth, the shrinking violet at any family gathering. Well, sure. She knew she was bringing to this union two illegitimate children, she knew she was five years older than Aaron, she knew she had nothing more than a high school education, she must have at least *suspected,* don't you think, must have at least had a faint *glimmer,* hmmm, that *some* of us in the Gulliver family (like me, for example) could see past the 36-C tits and shy batting eyelashes to where there lurked a conniving little country bitch intent on hitching her wagon to a future corporate star.

She dropped the pose the moment they were man and wife. That first year of their marriage, Gussie—we were still calling her Gussie back then—found some excuse to refuse, on behalf of herself, my brother, and her two delightful little girls, my mother's invitation to Grandma Rozalia's traditional Passover seder. Mind you, my mother's not religious. But Passover was important to Mom, as it was to all us kids when we were growing up, and still is, even now that Grandma Rozalia is dead. I wasn't married to Maggie the first time Augusta became a seder no-show, but in later years, even though she's not Jewish, Maggie attended each and every one of them, including the ones at my mother's house after Grandma died. In fact, Maggie told me she actually enjoyed them.

Not so Augusta.

Nor did she feel it was important to spend Thanksgiving with the Gullivers, or Christmas, which my mother also celebrated. She did come to my wedding because by then she must have sensed that I could become a formidable enemy, especially when twinned with my sister, but that was an exception. For all practical purposes, the day my brother married Augusta, he could have moved to China. My fondest wish is that one day I'll walk into a restaurant and see my brother sitting there with a gorgeous twenty-three-year-old natural blonde, not his wife.

I would cheer to the rafters.

I would buy him a cigar.

❑

My mother and I meet in front of the Metropolitan Museum, at twelve noon that Friday, and then walk into Central Park. This is the day after Independence Day and the park is unusually crowded, tourists and residents alike enjoying the long weekend.

My mother is wearing one of the Chanel ripoffs a tailor on Fifty-seventh Street makes for her. This one is fashioned of some light-weight fabric in the classic Chanel somewhat-plaid design. It fits her beautifully. Her auburn hair is neatly coiffed, her fingernails are painted a bright crimson. She takes good care of herself, my mother.

We sit in the sun on a park bench near a stately old maple. I have brought along sandwiches and Cokes I bought in a deli on Madison. I offer my mother a choice of either tuna and tomato on a hard roll or chicken salad on white. She opts for the chicken salad. I pop the can of

Coke for her, offer her a straw. We sit eating. Somewhere not too far away a man begins playing scales on a tuba. He makes his practicing sound like a symphony. It is a beautiful bright sunny day, and bloated fat notes float on the air. But we are here to discuss what we are going to do about a person who was declared schizophrenic not a week ago.

"Well, an Italian doctor," my mother says.

"Still, Mom . . ."

"In Sicily, no less. I've been to Sicily, thanks. You can have it. I can just imagine what kind of doctors they have there."

"That's why I think we ought to have her checked here."

"She'd never agree to seeing a psychiatrist. You know how she feels about the *health* care system, quote, unquote."

We have never been able to figure out why Annie thinks she knows something incriminating about the health care system. Something which, if she reported it to the proper authorities, would threaten the very foundations of our complacent society. It is true that when she was fourteen years old, during her summer vacation, she worked as a candy striper at Lenox Hill Hospital. But aside from this one supposedly "inside" look at health care, she has not been near a doctor or a dentist since. Well, except for the time she contracted malaria, and we had to take her to the hospital before she burned up alive or shook herself to death. Or—well, yes—the time she had what was diagnosed as an overdose of "something or other" by our then family doctor. But aside from those two instances, she has assiduously avoided any contact with members of the medical profession, who—like the shrink in Sicily—might falsely diagnose her as being . . . well . . . not normal.

"This may all be academic, anyway," my mother says. "She found a job."

"Are you serious?"

"I know, I'm even afraid to say it out loud."

"Where? What kind of job?"

"A jewelry store in Brooklyn. She'll be working behind the counter. It's only part-time, she'll be a salesperson. But at least it's something."

"It certainly is."

"She starts Saturday."

"That's really good news, Mom."

"Oh, please, I'm so *grateful*. But what I'm saying, Andrew, perhaps there's no need to do a follow-up here."

"I just thought a doctor here could . . ."

"You know how she feels about doctors."

"The point is, this'll be in her record forever," I tell my mother. "Unless a doctor here . . ."

"So? Who's going to look at her record? Is she applying for a job with NASA? She's content to make her own jewelry, open a little shop here or there, earn enough to get by on. That's all your sister needs."

"But she doesn't earn enough to get by on."

"Well."

"How much is this part-time job going to pay?"

"Well, not a lot. But it's something, Andrew. Don't belittle her efforts."

"I'm not. My point is, you keep giving her money, Mom."

"Am I supposed to let her starve? Be sensible, Andrew. With a little bit of money, Annie has always stayed productive and happy. That's all I wish for her. A wedding in June, forget it. She is what she is."

"But a doctor says she's . . ."

"A doctor in *Italy!* Do you put any store in what he said? Whatever his name is."

"Bertuzzi. Frankly, I don't know what to believe, Mom."

"Well, you met the man, you sat face to face with him. Did he seem . . . *authentic* to you?"

"He seemed like a doctor, yes. I mean, he wasn't rattling bones and throwing them in the dirt . . ."

My mother actually smiles.

" . . . he seemed like a genuine doctor in a respectable linen suit, yes."

"Did you see any diplomas on the wall? Any certificates? Anything like that?"

"No, Mom, I didn't. But he was a doctor, he was a psychiatrist, let's agree on that, can we? The question is what do we do now? A qualified psychiatrist has told us that Annie . . ."

"Does she look crazy to you?"

"No. But I'm not a . . ."

"She doesn't look crazy to me, either."

"Well, neither of us . . ."

"I think Annie is well aware of the consequences of what happened in Italy. If I can help her with enough money to live in decent housing, enough money for food and whatever supplies she needs to make her jewelry, maybe help her to open another little shop . . ."

"Aaron thinks she'll be running off again."

"Aaron is a wonderful son, but I don't think he's a very good brother. Don't you dare tell him I said that, Andrew," she warns and pats my hand playfully. "Didn't they give you any potato chips?" she asks.

"I think we ought to take her to a psychiatrist."

"Sure. While we're at it, let's take Hitler to a seder."

"If only to clear the record," I say, and suddenly my mother turns to me, her green eyes suspicious.

"And what else?" she asks.

"Nothing else. Set the record straight, get her a clean bill of health."

"And if not?"

"I'm not sure what you mean."

"Suppose a psychiatrist here *agrees* with this Bertuzzi, whatever his name is. What then? Do we put her in a strait jacket again?"

"They don't put people in strait jackets nowa . . ."

"They did in Italy!"

I sigh heavily. The man running scales on the tuba pauses and then begins again. I realize he is running chromatics. For an instant, it brings me back to the days when all we needed to be rock musicians was an electrical outlet and three chords.

"So what do you suggest instead, Mom? Give her another potful of money, send her on her . . ."

"I never give her that much money. Just enough to get by on. If I cut off her funds, then what? Do you want her to end up in a homeless shelter? Do you have any idea what that's like? It's a nightmare of theft, abuse, and drugs, is that what you want for your sister?"

"I want her to be happy and well," I say softly.

My mother turns to look at me again. Her eyes are relentless. Far away, the tuba player is doing the G scale.

"You *do* think she's crazy, don't you?" she says.

"I would like to find out if she is, Mom."

"She'll never agree to see a psychiatrist, forget it."

We are silent for several moments. The tuba player falls silent, too, resting. We sit in silence in golden sunshine in a park gone suddenly Seurat.

"I've already spoken to someone," I say.

"What do you mean?"

"A psychiatrist who was a friend of mine at NYU . . ."

"You talked to a *psychiatrist* without consulting . . . ?"

"Just for advice, Mom, okay? He specializes in psychopharmacology. He told me a long-lasting drug was probably administered to Annie by injection when she first arrived at the hospital, which is why she's still feeling so good. Plus the pills Bertuzzi prescribed. He said . . ."

"Yes, she *is* feeling good. In fact, I've never seen her . . ."

"He says there's no way to convince someone who's delusional . . ."

"Your sister is *not* delusional."

"*If* she's delusional, okay? There'd be no way to convince her she's not experiencing reality. He told me about this case where . . ."

"Your sister doesn't fit any of the . . ."

"Where this patient was convinced he was dead . . ."

"You're talking about very sick people here."

" . . . and his doctor tried to tell him otherwise, but the guy kept insisting he was dead, he was dead. So the doctor asked him if dead men bleed, and the patient said, 'No, of course not.' So the doctor pricked the man's finger with a pin, and of course he started bleeding. So the

25

doctor said, 'There. Does that prove anything to you?' And the patient looked at his finger, amazed, and said, 'Yes. I was wrong. Dead men *do* bleed.' "

"I don't see what that has to do with Annie."

"My friend thinks the best thing to do would be to put her in a psychiatric hospital . . ."

"Absolutely out of the question!"

" . . . for a few weeks . . ."

"Not for a *minute!*"

" . . . where she could work with someone, and develop a relationship, get her on treatment and medication. She has to realize from someone she trusts that she *was,* in fact, medicated in Italy, and she actually feels better now. You see, Mom, paranoid people . . ."

"Your sister's not paranoid."

"*If* she's paranoid, is what I'm saying. *If* she is, then she sees medication as just another plot to control her. He gave me the number of someone he thinks might be able to help her, a woman psychiatrist, he thinks she should see a woman . . ."

"She'd never agree."

"I think we should try."

"What you mean *we,* kemo sabe?" my mother says.

It is left for me to bell the cat.

❑

My sister and I are drinking coffee in the Starbucks on Seventieth and Broadway. It is three in the afternoon on a bright day in July. Annie has walked over from my mother's apartment. I have taken the subway uptown from my Chelsea apartment.

She is wearing a green sun dress that shows off to advantage the new tattoo on her left arm, a barbed-wire encirclement, or perhaps a ring of thorns, a tattoo I've seen on Puerto Rican gang members in the less than exemplary school at which I teach. Once, while I was serving on an after-school advisory committee two years ago, and trying to learn a little bit more about the kids we were supposed to be helping, I borrowed a book about juvenile delinquency from the library, and was surprised and delighted to learn that one of the chapters was titled "Twins: A Gang in Miniature."

We truly were a gang once, my sister and I.

About her tattoo, though, she tells me she had it done in a little shop in Palermo, and I see no reason to disbelieve her. According to Bertuzzi, there are bigger things my sister has to lie about. Or at least not understand the truth about. Then again, according to Bertuzzi, my sister is nuts.

But this is now the eighth day of July. We have been home for ten days now, and Annie hasn't tried to set fire to the apartment or shove anyone in front of a bus or jump off the roof. She is sipping a frappuccino. I am nursing a cappuccino without much foam. She seems perfectly all right. In fact, it is hard to believe Sicily ever happened. She seems to be the Annie I remember from our youth, a golden girl brimming with ideas, inventing word games, telling outrageous stories, doing hilarious and often cruel imitations of people we know.

On this sunny afternoon in July, she is telling me about a morning in Paris when she was having coffee at a little outdoor cafe in Montmartre, and seated at another table was this absolute stereotype of an Englishman, a Colonel Blimp if ever there was one—and here Annie puffs out her cheeks and raises her eyebrows and *becomes* this Englishman from Central Casting—this stout gentleman wearing a bowler, and carrying a cane, sitting there sipping his *café filtre,* his mustache bristling, sniffing the morning air and watching the French pass by on the sidewalk beyond. At long last, he turns to Annie, and says in round brown English tones, "Lovely morning, isn't it?" and Annie says, "Yes, lovely." He sips a bit more coffee, looks at the passing parade again, turns to Annie another time and says, "Lovely city, Paris." My sister nods, agrees, "Yes, lovely." He nods in return, studies the sidewalk again, turns to her yet another time, and says, "Lovely country, France." She says, "Yes, lovely," and he leans toward her and in a conspiratorial whisper says, "Pity it's wasted on the French."

I love my sister when she does accents.

We both burst out laughing, much to the annoyance of a stout woman sitting close to the air conditioner and trying to read Proust. Annie raises her eyebrows, and then does a quick impression of the scowling woman, which sets me off on another round of laughter, which causes me to choke on my cappuccino. The woman virtually snorts in disapproval. She snaps her book shut, gathers up her belongings, and storms out of the shop. Annie watches her go, imitating her waddle from the waist up. I keep laughing and choking and finally my sister says, "Are you all *right*, Andy?" and I tell her I'm fine, and begin laughing and choking all over again.

It is such a sweet warm July afternoon.

But I am waiting for the moment to tell her I think she should see a psychiatrist.

Annie falls silent, staring through the window at the sidewalk outside, nodding, smiling, presumably remembering that day in Paris and her conversation with the Englishman. But then, out of the blue, she says, "Go ahead, ask me."

"Ask you what, hon?"

"The answer is no," she says.

Has she read my mind?

"No, I'm not taking the medication that quack prescribed."

"Oh."

"Go ahead, yell at me."

"Why would I do that?"

"Maybe because you agree with him."

"Annie, more than anything else in the world, I want *not* to agree with him."

"Then stop watching me all the time," she says.

I was not aware that I'd been watching her. But perhaps I was. It occurs to me that ever since I spoke to Bertuzzi, I've been studying Annie for any indication that she may be listening to voices inside her head. We are silent for several moments. At last, I ask, "Well . . . how do you feel? When did you stop . . . ?"

"I stopped taking them a week ago. And I feel fine."

"Why'd you stop, Annie? You seemed to be . . ."

"There, you see? You're going to yell at me."

"Annie, please, I'm not going to yell at you. I'm just trying to find out . . ."

"Do you know what those pills were? A neuroleptic *drug*. Neuroleptic means 'affecting neurotransmissions,' I looked it up. Schizophrenia is a disease of the brain, you know, and several different neurotransmitter systems are believed to be involved in the dysfunction. Do I look as if I'm suffering from any goddamn neurotransmitter dysfunction?"

"You look fine to me, Annie."

"Yes, I *am* fine, thank you, and please don't bullshit me, Andy. You've been watching me like a hawk."

"I'm sorry, I didn't realize . . ."

"I stopped taking the pills because a) they were making me sleepy, and b) my face was twitching, and c) my arms and legs were beginning to feel stiff, and d) I'm not crazy. Any other questions?"

"No other questions, Annie. It's your life."

She turns to me sharply.

"What's that supposed to mean, Andy?"

"It's your life, you can do with it what you choose."

"That's exactly what I intend doing. As soon as I get past the trauma of being beaten and raped, I want to move on again."

"Okay."

"Sure, okay."

"I mean it, Annie. Whatever you want to do . . ."

"Sure, as long as I don't end up in another nuthouse, right?"

"Well, it was you who told them you were going to kill . . ."

"Yes, to save my *ass,* bro!"

"And it worked. But it *did* land you in a mental hospital."

"So?"

"So you ought to start thinking about that, is all I'm saying."

"Meaning?"

"Meaning you're almost thirty-six years old . . ."

"Please, not the white picket fence again."

"I'm not suggesting you get married . . ."

"Good, because there doesn't seem to be anyone who *wants* to marry me just now."

"But maybe you ought to think about settling down . . ."

"I was settled down in Maine for too damn . . ."

"Now that you have a job . . ."

"I quit the job. Didn't Mama tell you?"

"No, she didn't. Why'd you quit?"

"It wasn't right for me. I make jewelry, Andy. That's my job. I'm an artist, Andy. I make fine jewelry."

"I know you do."

"So why should I work in somebody else's shop? I've had my *own* shops, Andy. It's not my fault people don't appreciate my work."

"You do beautiful work, Annie."

"Thank you. Even if you don't mean it."

"I do mean it."

"Thanks."

We fall silent again. I sip at the cappuccino. I hate cappuccino without foam.

"You know, if what happened is still bothering you . . ."

"Of *course* it's bothering me! Wouldn't it bother you? Getting beaten and raped?"

"That's what I'm saying. You said you wanted to get past it . . ."

"Oh, boy, do I!"

"So maybe you ought to, you know, talk to someone about it."

"Like who?" she says at once. "Another quack like Bertuzzi?"

"No, I was thinking . . ."

"No psychiatrists, Andy! Absolutely not!"

"Well, there are psychiatrists and there are psychiatrists," I say. "I'm sure we could find someone who's used to dealing with . . . you know . . . rape victims."

"What good would that do?"

"Well . . . you could, you know, get it off your chest."

"Is a psychiatrist going to correct the false accusations Bertuzzi made about me?"

"I'm sure if you told someone . . ."

"Otherwise what's the use? The man was part of a determined conspiracy to cover up the indignities I suffered at the hands of an inept health care system. Instead of talking to another psychiatrist, I should be talking to someone in the State Department. Get *them* to make the proper inquiries in Italy, clear the record there."

"Well, I don't think that would be possible, Annie."

"Of course not. Schizophrenic! I get furious every time I think about it."

"You could discuss that, too. Your anger. You could set the matter straight in your own mind, come to terms with . . ."

"There's nothing wrong with my *mind*, bro! I just don't want the word 'schizophrenic' following me around *America's* health care system. The health care system here is bad enough as it is, don't get me started on the health care system here in America. It's what I *know* about the health care system that probably caused all that trouble in Sicily, don't get me started."

"But you know," I say, "there's nothing to be afraid of, really. All you have to do . . ."

"Why would I be afraid of anything?"

"That's just what I'm saying. If we find the right person . . . a woman maybe . . . someone who's had experience with rape victims . . . then all you have to do is tell the truth. Set the record straight, you know?"

Annie looks at me.

"What harm can it do?" I ask.

She nods. A calculating look settles into her eyes.

Is she listening to her voices? I wonder. Are they advising her to run for the hills? Or are they working out a defense?

"Let's get out of here," she says. "It's warm in here, don't you think it's warm in here?"

31

❑

We are walking in Central Park, my sister and I.

My father used to take us to the park all the time when we were young. We are walking there without my father now, of course, and without Aaron either. It is just the two of us. The Twins. "Where are The Twins?" my mother used to say. Or "Go get The Twins." Or "Tell The Twins it's bedtime." Always The Twins. An entity. Annie and I. The Twins.

We are strolling along in the sunshine, holding hands actually, the way we used to when we were a gang in miniature, when suddenly she says, as if affirming something she's been thinking about all along, "I could tell her about the pony ride."

I don't know what she's talking about.

Or is she talking to me?

Oh, Jesus, is she consulting with her goddamn voices?

"The pony ride," she says, turning to me. We are still holding hands. "You weren't there," she says. "It was at Grandma Rozalia's house."

My grandmother used to have a house in New Rochelle. My mother took us there a lot after my father abandoned us. I guess maybe he did truly abandon us in that we never heard from him again. That is to say, he duly divorced my mother, and paid alimony and child support, but he never tried to see either Aaron, or me, or my sister. I often wonder how a person can do that. Never see his own children again. Sometimes, I'm happy Maggie and I never had kids.

Anyway, my grandmother Rozalia was Hungarian, like my grandfather Aaron, but she used to smoke these cigarettes she imported from France. She used to smoke them in a long cigarette holder. She had long black hair and cushiony breasts, and she would stand by the fireplace in the front room of her New Rochelle house and smoke her cigarettes like a countess or something. Annie used to play with her dolls and I used to build Lego houses by the fire while the grownups talked about important matters. When we got older, Annie used to tease my grandmother all the time. Whenever she wanted to really get her goat, she would ask, "Grandma, how do you make Hungarian chicken soup?" and my grandmother would say, "Get out of here, you," and wave her away with a hand covered with diamonds, and Annie would say, "First you steal a chicken," and Grandma would laugh each and every time. I don't know why I wasn't at Grandma's house that day of the pony ride—if it ever happened. Maybe I was at a Yankee's game with Aaron. It was only a short subway ride to the Bronx, and my mother let us go alone all the time. We never got molested or anything.

This man came around with his pony at around three in the afternoon. It was a brown and white Shetland with a big saddle on it so that two kids could take a ride at the same time, one behind the other. The man was wearing a ragged straw hat, sandals, baggy blue trousers, and a bright green, short-sleeved shirt with a little blue sweater vest open over it. He charged a dollar to take the kids once around the block on his pony. When my sister saw him outside through the lace curtains in Grandma's front room, she started dancing up and down and begging Grandma to let her go on the pony, please. Grandma finished her cigarette and then took my sister outside and watched while the grizzled old man in the straw hat lifted first Annie onto the saddle, and then an eleven-year-old boy Annie had never seen before in her life.

"The old man copped a feel when he lifted me onto the saddle," she tells me now.

"What do you mean? You were only seven. What was there to feel?"

"He slipped his hand under my dress. Onto my panties. He patted my ass."

"Come on, Annie."

"He did. Would I lie about something like that?"

"Well, no, but . . ."

But yes, according to Bertuzzi, Annie has lied—or at least distorted the truth—often enough to warrant a diagnosis of schizophrenia. Hallucinations, he called them. Delusions, he called them. So why not now? Why not lie—or at least distort the truth—about a man who gave her a goddamn pony ride when she was seven? She has stopped taking her medication. Why *not* sail off into Looneyland again? If ever she'd been there at all. Why *not* listen to whatever voices are now concocting this cockamamie story about child abuse?

"Maybe that's what gave that kid the idea," she says.

"What kid? Who do you mean?"

"The kid behind me on the pony. He got a hard-on," she tells me.

"That's okay, I don't want to hear it," I say, and I drop her hand.

"That's why I ended up in that hospital in Italy," she says.

I say nothing.

"Because he put his hand under my dress and got a hard-on. I thought that ride would never end. The old man kept leering at me all the while this fat little bastard kept prodding me from behind with his silly little prick. I think he came on the back of my panties, yes. My panties were all sticky when I got off that horse, that pony. I think he must have come on me. I'd like to tell someone about this, Andy. I really think it's the source of all my problems."

I think, Oh, Jesus, they've convinced her she can fool a psychiatrist!

"My inability to communicate with people of the opposite sex," she says. "Except you, of course, I can tell you anything."

Yes, anything. Except the fact that this isn't you talking, this is whoever's inside your head, inventing a story you can try on a psychiatrist, if ever we get to see one, which is unlikely since it's not you making these decisions, Annie, it's your goddamn voices!

"My inability to socialize," she says. "To form commitments. I think it all goes back to when I was seven years old and took that pony ride, I really do. I'd like to tell someone about it, Andy. I'd like to get to the bottom of it."

"Well . . . who do you mean, honey?"

"Can you find a holistic psychiatrist?" she asks.

I catch my breath.

"I won't take any more medicines, Andy. If you can't find someone who . . ."

"I think I can find someone," I say.

"Good," she says, and takes my hand in hers again.

❏

The last day of July dawns clear and bright and breezy.

I take the subway uptown from Chelsea and arrive at my mother's apartment at nine o'clock sharp. My sister is dressed casually, which I think might be a good sign. No starched blouse and pleated skirt, no ribbons in her hair. Instead, she is wearing faded jeans and a white T-shirt (no bra, I notice), the barbed-wire tattoo showing on the bicep of her left arm. She asks if we have time for a cup of coffee, and we sit together in the little windowed alcove in my mother's apartment, the three of us sipping coffee and eating toasted bagels, and talking about how surprisingly cool it is for the end of July. My mother looks apprehensive. I sometimes think she is as frightened of psychiatrists as Annie is. But my sister seems cheerful and unafraid, and I begin thinking, Gee, maybe she *is* only neurotic, maybe some son of a bitch or bitches *did* actually molest her when she was seven years old, maybe the doctor in Sicily *was* wrong, maybe my poor dear beloved sister is in fact a victim.

We sit in glowing sunshine eating bagels and sipping coffee.

It is a hopeful morning.

❏

Dr. Sarah Lang is a not unattractive woman in her early fifties, I guess, wearing her gone-to-white hair shoulder length, wearing as well black-rimmed eyeglasses that frame and highlight the effect of her vivid blue eyes.

"Miss Gulliver?" she asks.

"Yes?" Annie says.

"Did you want to come in, please?"

"I want my brother to come in with me, if that's all right," Annie says.

Dr. Lang looks at me.

"I can wait out here," I say, "that's okay."

"I want you to hear this," Annie says.

Dr. Lang looks from one to the other of us.

"Would that be all right?" Annie asks.

"It's your nickel," Dr. Lang says, and smiles.

Annie smiles back.

"So come in," Dr. Lang says. "Both of you. Please."

The windows in her office face north on Ninety-sixth Street. This is ten in the morning; the light is oblique. There is a desk with some papers on it. There are diplomas hanging on the walls, nothing else. Three or four diplomas from various universities and medical schools. No framed paintings. Just the diplomas and a license to practice psychiatry in the state of New York, and a commendation of some sort from a psychiatric society. There is a long leather couch to the right of the desk, but Dr. Lang motions to two matching leather chairs slightly to the left, and my sister and I sit facing her.

"So," she says, "what's this you want both of us to hear?"

"I was molested," Annie says.

Dr. Lang nods.

"When I was eleven years old," Annie says.

And now comes the second version of the story.

In this version, the super is upstairs fixing a leak in the plumbing under the kitchen sink. Annie is home with a cold. My brother and I are off at school. My mother has gone downstairs to Gristede's, to pick up some soup for lunch. Annie is watching television. She remembers exactly what she was watching. She tells Dr. Lang and me that she was watching a re-run of *Lassie*. She also remembers what Mr. Alvarez was wearing on that fateful July morning.

Mr. Alvarez is wearing baggy blue trousers and a little blue sweater vest, a shabby straw hat he takes off and rests on the counter top before he crawls under the sink, and a green, short-sleeved shirt open at the throat to reveal a gold crucifix nestling in curly black hairs on his chest and creeping up to his Adam's apple. He has a tattoo on the bicep of his left arm, Jesus Christ's red heart encircled by a crown of blue thorns.

"Little girl?" he says.

She is not sure at first that anyone is actually calling to her. She is lying on the sofa in the living room, her eyes glued to the TV screen where the family has come out on the porch and is yelling for Lassie, when she hears this voice calling "Little girl?" or actually "Little *gorl?*" was probably more like it, since Mr. Alvarez's accent was as thick as a Colombian rain forest. She thinks at first that it is a voice coming from the TV set, someone calling to her from somewhere in the episode she's watching, or rather calling to someone actually *in* the episode, one of the actors, a member of the family that owns Lassie, but certainly not a voice calling to her from under the kitchen sink.

"Little gorl?" he says again, and this time she realizes the voice is actually in the apartment with her and not being beamed from somewhere out in Televisionland, actually coming from under the sink, actually coming from Mr. Alvarez under the sink in his baggy blue pants and short-sleeved green shirt and little blue sweater vest. Annie herself is wearing a short cotton nightgown with red check cotton panties and over that the bathrobe Grandma Rozalia gave her for her tenth birthday last year. She is also wearing bedroom slippers that have bunny faces on them, and little bunny ears sticking up. The slippers are purple, and she knows they don't match the nightgown or the robe or for that matter the red check panties. This bothers her a little. That the slippers don't match anything.

"Little gorl, come here a secon'," Mr. Alvarez says.

She gets off the couch reluctantly—Lassie is just about to rescue someone from drowning, if she remembers correctly, or perhaps from a burning building—and she slouches into the kitchen where the straw hat with its uneven edges is resting on the counter top catching sunlight. She cannot see Mr. Alvarez's face. He is under the sink. She sees only his arm with its heart and thorns tattoo, and his outstretched hand.

"The wrench," he says. "In my box."

She sees his open tool box on the floor, and inside it she sees a variety of screw drivers and hammers and wrenches and other tools, she doesn't know what they are. She stands there puzzled, wondering which wrench she should hand him. She is about to ask him which wrench he means, when she feels his hand sliding up the inside of her leg.

She stands stock still.

"He shoved aside my panties and stuck his finger inside me," my sister tells Dr. Lang. "I wet my pants. I peed on his hand."

"That must have been awful for you," Dr. Lang says.

"It was. Oh, you'd better believe it. It's what caused all that trouble in Italy."

I do not for a moment believe that Annie is going to reveal she was in a nuthouse in Italy. I know my sister better than that. She is here today to get to the bottom of things, to set the record straight. She is here today because kindly Mr. Alvarez molested her, and as a result she has behaved strangely for the past twenty-five years. She is not nuts, she is merely neurotic.

"What trouble in Italy?" Dr. Lang asks.

"I was hospitalized in Italy," Annie says, and nods.

But this is not what she'd been rehearsing! Have the voices changed their mind? *Her* mind? Have the voices advised her to change her mind? Are the voices themselves beginning to lose it?

"Oh?" Dr. Lang says.

"Well, I wouldn't say 'hospitalized,' actually," Annie says at once. "I was *taken* to a hospital, yes, but I wouldn't say I was 'hospitalized' as such."

"Why were you taken to a hospital?"

"Because I was bruised and bleeding."

Dr. Lang nods. Smiles. Waits.

"I was attacked." Annie hesitates. "I was raped and beaten. That's why they took me to a hospital."

"Which hospital was this?" Dr. Lang asks.

"Ospedale Santa Chiara," she says. "In Sicily. Do you know it?"

"I'm sorry, no."

Annie hesitates, and then says, "It's a pediatric hospital."

"I see. They took you to a pediatric hospital."

"Well, yes. It's all they had. It isn't New York, you know."

"I can imagine. How long were you there?"

"In Sicily? Almost two months. I'd spent some time in . . ."

"The hospital, I mean."

"Oh. A week."

"They kept you there a week."

"Yes. Well, I was waiting for Andy to get there."

"Your brother."

"Yes. Andy," she says, and turns to look at me.

"I'm sorry, I'm not sure I understand. Why was your brother coming there?"

"To get me."

"Why did he have to come get you? Were you injured very badly?"

"Well, they had to release me."

"Yes, I understand. But why did your brother . . . ?"

"He had to sign some papers."

"What sort of papers?"

"Release papers."

"Couldn't you sign them yourself?"

"That's just what *I* said! They told me someone had to sign for me."

"Why?"

Annie thinks for a moment. Her eyes actually narrow. The calculating look is there again. I wonder if there are truly voices inside her head. If so, are they now telling her what to say to the doctor?

Is there only one voice?

Watch it, Annie! She's getting close, she knows you were in the psychiatric wing! Tell her you had a broken leg!

More than one voice?

She's not handling this properly.

I know, she's never very good with doctors.

In fact, she's never very good with anyone.

In fact, she's utterly worthless.

Auditory hallucinations. One of the Criterion-A symptoms. Either a single voice keeping up a running commentary on the person's behavior, or two or more voices conversing with each other.

"What happened," Annie says, "was these two boys tried to pick up my friend and me in this little bar in town."

Dr. Lang is nodding. No longer smiling. Just nodding. She doesn't yet know Annie was in a mental hospital, so far all Annie's told her is that it was a pediatric hospital. Annie is still telling the story she told me on the phone from Italy, the story she again told the gathered family once she was safe again in New York, objecting strenuously whenever any of us asked for clearer details—

"Why are you second-guessing me?" she would shout. "I refuse to be second-guessed!"

In retrospect, I think she meant that we were cross-examining her. I think she meant to say, "I refuse to be cross-examined!" No one is cross-examining her now. Dr. Lang is merely listening.

"Well, we didn't *wish* to be picked up, thank you," Annie says, "and this led to a little argument, and I suppose it got out of hand."

"How?"

"One of the boys got violent. He grabbed a bottle of wine from the table, grabbed it by the neck, and swung it at me. Spilled red wine all over the white cotton dress I was wearing. So naturally, I fought back. Then Lise and I, that's this German girl I was traveling with, ran out of the place, and somehow we got separated, and I found myself on this mountain road being followed by banditos—look, it's a long story, and there's no point telling it all over again, you'll only try second-guessing me, anyway, so what's the use? The point is, I ended up in the hospital because I was raped and robbed and because the police wouldn't do anything about it. And I'm sure this relates back to having been a victim when I was only eleven, they can sense that about a person, you know, the predators out there. They can smell a victim a hundred yards away. So I played a trick on them—which led them to the wrong conclusion later on, of course—but it worked, it got me in the hospital where at least I was safe till Andy came to get me out."

She nods in satisfaction, folds her hands in her lap.

"What trick was that?" Dr. Lang asks.

"What?"

"This trick you played."

Be careful, Annie, she's closing in.

Annie shrugs.

"You said you played a trick on them . . ."

She's about to blow it.

She's never any good with doctors.

"Can you tell me what the trick was?"

"I told them I'd kill myself," Annie says.

"Really?" Dr. Lang asks.

"Sure," Annie says, pleased with herself, smiling now. "Well, they weren't going to help me unless I took desperate measures."

"So you said you'd kill yourself if they didn't help you?"

"It was all I could think of."

"Did you mean it?"

"Of course not! It was a desperation measure, I just told you."

"But I can understand how it led them to the wrong conclusion later on, can't you?"

"Oh, sure. They thought I was nuts."

"I can see why they might have thought that."

"But it was just a trick."

"So how did they treat you? Once you got to the hospital?"

"Very nicely, actually. It was a pediatric hospital. There were women giving birth every . . ."

"I meant . . . what treatment did they give you? You said they thought you were nuts . . ."

"That's no surprise. My whole family thinks I'm nuts."

"Is that so?"

"Sure."

"Why do you suppose that is?"

"I have no idea. Everyone else thinks I'm in amazing mental and physical shape."

"How old are you, Annie?"

"I'll be thirty-six in September. Everyone I spend time with thinks

I'm extremely happy and intelligent. It's just my family who keep watching me like a hawk. I *burp* and they think that's a sign of mental illness. I was initiated into Tantric yoga quite some time ago, you know. I know my brother doesn't believe in God . . ."

A sidelong glance at me.

" . . . but I do believe in God, and I'm in continual devotional practice which my family somehow interprets as suffering. I'm not suffering. I'm healthy and happy."

"Then why are you here today?" Dr. Lang asks.

"Tantra is all about understanding yourself. I'm trying to completely digest all the implications and ramifications of what happened to me when I was eleven. I'm trying to free myself from that unpleasant trauma. I don't think that's an unreasonable expectation, do you? I mean, it seems absolutely clear to me that if I don't try to help myself, no one else is going to help me."

Another sidelong glance at me.

This time, Dr. Lang picks up on it.

"Do you mean your brother?"

"For all I know, he's part of it."

"Part of what?"

"Ask him."

"Well, I'd rather know what you think."

"He's never there when I get in trouble. He always manages to be someplace else. Don't you think that's odd?"

"I don't understand. You didn't expect him to be there in *Italy,* did you? When those boys . . ."

"Of course not."

"Then when *did* you expect him to be there?"

"I *don't* expect him to be there, forget it. I don't expect him to be *anywhere,* forget it. In fact, I don't even know why *I'm* here."

"You said you wanted to free yourself from . . ."

"Yes, well, *that* was a big mistake, wasn't it?"

"What do you mean?"

"I mean, I don't like being second-guessed."

"Second-guessed?"

"Second-guessed, second-guessed. Why do you want to know how I was treated in that hospital, that *prison* is what it was. They put me in a strait jacket, is how I was treated. They molested me while I was tied to the bed. They gave me a very mild dosage of a tranquilizer called Risperdal. After what happened to me, and the way I must have looked to them, all battered and bruised and bleeding—and remember, I told them I'd kill myself, don't forget that—I'm not *surprised* they thought I needed a tranquilizer. Are you familiar with Risperdal?"

"Yes, I am. It's used to manage psychotic disorders."

"No, you're confusing it with Haldol. I had no symptoms of any psychotic disorder in Italy. None at all. I can *prove* that to you. I was given Risperdal, not Haldol, you ought to check your pharmacology, Doctor. In any case, I was initiated into the practice of Kundalini yoga a long time ago, through the direct transmission of Shaktipat from the guru, and sometimes adepts will exhibit side effects and strange behavior. If my family thinks such behavior is a sign of a serious mental condition, then it's because they're misinformed or uneducated or both. I'm here to set the record straight. I refuse to be second-guessed, and I refuse to be the victim of my family's obsessive attachment to labeling me an ill person. Is that clear?"

"I quite understand, yes," Dr. Lang says, and looks at the small silver Tiffany clock on her desk. "Well," she says, "I think our time is up. Let me give your brother a call, all right? Sometime next week, Mr. Gulliver, hmm?"

But next week is now.

And Annie is gone.

3

We call Bellevue. Or rather, I do. They have no record of a patient named Anne Rozalia Gulliver having been admitted that night. Rozalia is my sister's middle name. It was my grandmother Lederer's name, too, as you know. My sister despises it. *My* middle name is Robert, which is no winner, either, but it was my grandfather Gulliver's name. Anne Rozalia Gulliver and Andrew Robert Gulliver. Twins, of course, though not identical, and named like twins, though not identically.

We were so much alike when we were young.

In high school, I once played Mortimer Brewster in a production of *Arsenic and Old Lace*. No, I'm not an actor, although my mother tried to encourage such a pursuit. I am merely a school teacher. Anyway, there's a line in the play, where Mortimer is trying to explain his family to his girlfriend Elaine. When I delivered the line, I thought it was funny. The audience thought so, too. The scene—I still remember it—goes like this:

MORTIMER

I love you very much, Elaine. In fact, I love you so
much I can't marry you.

ELAINE

Have you suddenly gone crazy?

MORTIMER

I don't think so, but it's just a matter of time. You see,
insanity runs in my family. It practically gallops. That's
why I can't marry you, dear.

It practically gallops.

The audience fell down laughing.

It practically gallops.

My brother Aaron doesn't like to think insanity practically gallops in
our family. His two adopted daughters are immune, of course, but suppose he himself should one day begin brushing imaginary cockroaches
off the coverlet, an unlikelihood at his age, but, listen, who can tell?

I put the phone receiver back on its cradle.

"She's not at Bellevue," I say.

"I think we should call the police," Augusta suggests.

"No police," my mother says flatly. "I don't want Annie ending up
in another lunatic asylum. She isn't psychotic."

"The doctor in Sicily told Andy . . ."

"Some doctor."

"If a goddamn psychiatrist flatly states . . ."

"I'm not interested in what he stated. And watch your language,
Miss."

"In fact, we should have called the police years ago."

"What's that supposed to mean?"

"Calm down, you two, okay?" Aaron says.

"When you live with a person closely," my mother says, quite
evenly, "you get to know that person pretty well, even if she is your
own daughter. Annie functions fine on her own . . ."

"Still," Augusta says, "we can't dismiss the fact . . ."

"*Normally*," my mother says, raising her voice, "she functions well on her own. She is capable of making and executing plans . . ."

"Which sometimes get her in trouble," Aaron says.

"Not very often," my mother says.

"Often enough," Augusta says. "She just landed herself in a Sicilian hospital . . ."

"That is a rare instance."

" . . . where she was diagnosed as schizophrenic."

"Nonsense," my mother says. "If I had to characterize her, I'd say she's an artistically obsessed religious zealot."

"Then maybe she's hiding out in St. Patrick's Cathedral," Augusta says. "Or the Museum of Modern Art."

I hate it when my sister-in-law tries to be funny about Annie. I think she does this only to gain further favor with Aaron, who by the way has never thought any of our sister's little escapades were in the slightest bit comical, even when they really were. As for example, the time she peed on a cop's shoes in Georgia.

"Or maybe we ought to go look for her guru," Augusta adds, compounding the felony.

"Augusta, you're not being funny," I say.

"Tell her," my mother says.

"We're trying to figure out what to do here, and you . . ."

"All right, all right," Augusta says, and waves her hands on the air.

"If Annie really tries to hurt someone . . ."

"She won't hurt anyone," my mother says.

"You don't know that, Mom."

"I know she hasn't hurt anyone *so far*."

I give my mother a look, but say nothing.

❑

We spend the next hour or so calling every hospital in New York City. My mother has only one line going into her apartment, so we take turns on the phone. There are thirty or so general hospitals in Manhattan, and another fifty or more in the other four boroughs. We call the ones in Manhattan first, because we figure if Annie's going to get in trouble it'll be right here in the city and not anywhere else.

Augusta, by the way, still doesn't know that to anyone born and bred in New York, Manhattan is "the city." If somebody living in the Bronx is going downtown to see a Broadway show, he says he's going "into the city," even though technically, the Bronx is part of the city as well. Augusta was born in Ridley Hills, New Jersey, where she was the belle of the ball and the delight of the Ridley Royals. She doesn't know from city streets. I know she hates my sister, and won't allow her to set foot in her house. Maybe that's why I dislike her so intensely.

She now keeps insisting that we call the police. Mama will hear of no such thing. After what happened in Sicily, she is afraid Annie will end up in some mental institution again, in a strait jacket, banging her head against the wall and sitting in her own shit. They will perform electro-convulsive therapy on her, and immerse her in hot or cold baths, and eventually they will do a prefrontal lobotomy and turn her into a fucking vegetable.

Sometimes, I, too, believe this will happen to my poor dear sister. And it frightens me.

❏

It is Augusta's turn on the phone now. When she has called ten hospitals in Manhattan, one of us will relieve her, and begin calling the next ten. Meanwhile, we are trying to dope out where Annie might have gone.

"I just hope she isn't already on a plane to Timbuktu," my mother says.

"Did you give her money again?" I ask.

"No. But there's nothing wrong with giving her money."

"After Sicily, I would have hoped . . ."

"Forget Sicily. You're obsessed with Sicily. What happened there is not representative."

"Maybe we should call the airports, anyway," Aaron suggests. "In case she got hold of some money somehow."

"Oh, she knows how to get hold of money, all right," Augusta says, and rolls her eyes.

"Well, let's finish with the hospitals first," I say.

"You really should put in a second line," Aaron tells my mother.

"Sure, and who'll pay for it?"

"It would come in handy in emergencies like this."

"This isn't an emergency," my mother says. "Annie's gone away before. She's always managed to take care of herself and come back safely."

"This is a waste of time," Augusta says, and puts the phone back on its cradle. "It's four in the morning, all I'm getting are nurses' aides with Spanish accents."

"Nobody speaks English in this city anymore," my mother says.

"Must be a conspiracy, Mom."

"Tell me about it, Andrew."

"Augusta's right," Aaron says, ever to the rescue. "Annie isn't in any hospital, she's just hiding. As usual."

"You know that for a fact, huh, Aaron?" I say.

"I'm basing it on empirical knowledge. She has never tried to hurt herself, so why are we calling every damn hospital in the city? We called Bellevue, that should be enough."

"By the time we call all these hospitals," Augusta says, "she could be on her way to God knows where."

I'm beginning to think they're right. If Annie, God forbid, got hit by a bus, and they took her to the nearest hospital, they'd immediately discover she was nuts—if, in fact, she is—and transfer her to Bellevue, wouldn't they? But we ourselves have been living with her strange behavior ever since she was sixteen, and none of us ever thought she was truly sick until Bertuzzi in Sicily laid all the cards on the table, and called a spade a spade. It's possible, then, that she's already in some hospital out there, suffering from a broken leg or a nose bleed, and no one has yet recognized that she may need . . . well . . . psychiatric help.

"Maybe we ought to call Dr. Lang," I suggest.

"A lot of good she did," my mother says. "Annie's run off again, hasn't she? Don't you have a cell phone, Aaron? President of a big corporation? Your brother, I can understand . . ."

Meaning I am but a mere teacher of English in the New York City school system.

"But *you?* Even Annie has a cell phone. You really should get a cell phone."

"Maybe we *should* call that shrink," Augusta says.

"Why?" my mother asks.

"Well, first of all," I say, "I'd like to hear her evaluation of . . ."

"I wouldn't."

"She may have some insights into . . ."

"You shouldn't have gone to her in the first place."

"It was Annie's suggestion, Mom."

"*You* chose the doctor."

"Annie *asked* me to find one."

"With a little noodge from her brother, hmm?"

"Mom, she told me she wanted to . . ."

"Sure, and you listened to her. A person who'd just been through a traumatic experience in Italy . . ."

"Where she was diagnosed as schizophrenic, by the way," Augusta says.

"Thank you for reminding us of that again, darling."

"I merely speak the truth," Augusta says, and shrugs.

"Hey, everybody, knock if off, okay?" Aaron says.

"I don't see any harm in calling Dr. Lang."

"She'll just want to lock your sister up again."

"I didn't get the impression . . ."

"Psychiatrists."

" . . . that she wanted to lock Annie up, Mom."

"It was a psychiatrist who locked her up in Sicily, wasn't it?"

"I'm going downstairs for a cigarette," Augusta says.

"Sure, smoke yourself to death," my mother says.

"I'll see you later," Augusta says, and takes her handbag, and heads for the front door.

"I'll come with you," Aaron says, "this neighborhood."

"There's nothing wrong with this neighborhood!" my mother says.

"I meant, this hour of the night."

"*Any* hour of the night!" my mother snaps, and cuts him a sharp look, but he doesn't notice, he's already out the door. Besides, we both know his going downstairs has nothing to do with the neighborhood. He is going down to have a smoke with Augusta. Five years ago, he told us he quit smoking. We both know this is a lie because even his clothes smell of tobacco. But he keeps up the pretense because he thinks it improves his stature in our eyes. He knows I can't stand Augusta. And he knows that however much he may achieve professionally, he will never quite earn Mama's approval. In that respect, Aaron and I are in the very same boat. Mama doesn't think much of my professional status, either. Then again, I haven't ever really achieved anything.

Once upon a time, I wanted to be a writer.

Before my father left, he used to read to me and Annie and Aaron at bedtime. One of our favorite books was *The Once and Future King*. Annie loved all the parts where Merlin changes the Wart into a fish and all kinds of flying birds and finally a badger. I liked the Wart's adventures with Robin Wood, which of course was the legendary Robin Hood's true and honorable name. Listening to my father read to us, I thought if I could ever write like T. H. White, I would be the happiest person in the entire world. Then my father left home, and from what I could gather he had gone to live with his mother for a while, so I wrote him a letter and asked my mother to mail it to him.

The letter read:

Dear Daddy,

Mom says you are with Grandma Kate. I miss you and love you very much. Please come home.

Your loving son,
Andrew

He never came home.

I sometimes wonder if my mother ever mailed that letter.

❑

The crying was one thing.

When I stopped eating, that was another story.

I was never a picky eater until my father left home. Then everything seemed to taste rotten.

One night, I was playing in the living room with this dart set my grandmother sent me for my sixth birthday—we weren't allowed to see Grandma Kate anymore, but she still sent us gifts, which my mother didn't dare keep from us.

The dart set had a target with circles on it and a bull's eye and six darts with different colored feathers on them for different players. I put the target on a piece of plywood so the darts wouldn't damage anything if I missed. My mother was already annoyed that Grandma Kate had sent me a game with pointed things in it; she'd have taken a fit if I threw a dart and wrecked a wall or a piece of furniture.

When she called us in to dinner, Aaron came from where he was pounding on the piano, and Annie came from where she was playing with one of her dolls, and I came in from practicing darts, carrying one of the darts with me, the one with the red feathers. I was sort of twirling the dart around on my fingers when my mother came in with our dinner. She prided herself on her cooking, my mother did. She cooked about as well as Aaron played piano, but all her friends kept telling her she was a terrific cook.

That night, she was serving these thick veal chops Aaron loved, with mashed potatoes and creamed spinach she made herself that wasn't frozen. She had just put everything on the table when a fly started buzzing around the kitchen. This was an old apartment, what they called pre-war, and it had no air-conditioning, which meant we kept the windows open winter and summer, though not as much in the winter, and there were flies in it year round.

Through the open doorway connecting kitchen and dining room, I watched the fly as it landed first on the refrigerator and then the cookie jar in the shape of a pig on the counter near the stove, and then zipped out of the kitchen and into the dining room and landed on the wall someplace behind me. I whirled around in my chair and without even taking aim, threw the dart, and hit the fly smack behind its head, pinning it to the wall. A gooey white fluid came oozing out of the fly, and I went "Ick!" and turned back to the table to find sitting in front of me a big bowl of mashed potatoes that looked just like the gooey white stuff coming out of the fly.

My mother didn't know I'd nailed a fly to the wall with what had to be the luckiest shot in all New York City, even better than a bull's eye. She'd been busy running in and out of the kitchen carrying platters and plates and now she saw me looking down at the bowl of mashed potatoes she'd worked very hard to make creamy and smooth, and she saw me pulling a face, and heard me saying "Ick!" and she said at once, "What now?" because ever since I'd stopped crying over my father leaving, I'd been a pain in the ass about eating.

"I don't want any potatoes," I said, and Aaron said, "He just killed a fly," and my mother said, "Shut up, Aaron," and then, to me, "Why not?" and I said, "They're icky," and Annie said, "You should've seen it, Mom!" and my mother said, "Shut up, Annie," and to me, "Icky? *Icky?*" and Aaron said, "Can we start eating, Mom?" and my mother said, "Shut up, Aaron!" and picked up the bowl of potatoes in both hands and dumped it onto my head. Just turned the bowl over on my head like a helmet.

The potatoes were every bit as creamy and as smooth as my mother might have hoped. They streamed over my forehead and into my eyes and down my cheeks and mouth and dripped from my chin. I began crying again, the way I had after my father left. "And I've had enough of that goddamn *crying!*" my mother shouted. "Go to your room!" My sister started crying, too. "And you, too, you little pisspants!" my mother shouted.

I went first to the bathroom where I wiped off my face with toilet paper and then washed it and dried it with a towel, and then went into my room where I discovered there was mashed potato all over my pants, too. I wiped that off with my handkerchief before I got undressed. Then I crawled into bed, and cried myself to sleep. Next door, I could hear Annie crying, too.

Aaron and my mother ate dinner alone that night.

The next morning, I was afraid to talk to her.

❑

When Annie, Aaron, and I were kids, we used to hide under the dining room table, eavesdropping on the conversation of the grownups. Once we heard Grandma Kate use the word "shit," and we burst out laughing, and Mama sent all of us to our rooms—but she was laughing, too. This was before my father abandoned us. The moment he was gone, my mother changed a lot. It was like night and day. Two different people. Aaron told us she was grieving. Neither Annie nor I knew what grieving meant.

She never took us to see Grandma Kate anymore.

She told us that when Daddy abandoned us, it was the same thing as Grandma Kate abandoning us. It was the whole Gulliver family that had abandoned us. Annie told her she loved Grandma Kate and Aunt Tess and Uncle Mike, and she didn't know why she couldn't see them anymore. My mother told her to shut up, we can't see them anymore, and that's *that!*

"What do you mean, we can't see them?" Annie asked. "Did they disappear? Like Merlin?"

"Just be quiet," my mother said.

"Regular people can't disappear, can they?" Annie asked me.

"I don't think so."

"Regular people can't disappear," Annie told my mother.

"That's right, they can't," Aaron said. "So shut up."

"Did Daddy disappear?"

"Daddy abandoned us," my mother said.

"What's abandon?"

"It means he went away forever," Aaron said.

"He did not," Annie said.

"Yes, he did," my mother said, and I burst into tears.

On Thanksgiving Day that year . . .

There was some kind of mixup on Thanksgiving Day.

I can remember playing jacks with Annie in her room (she always cheated, making up rules and then changing them five minutes later) and hearing my mother shouting to all us kids to come have breakfast. Aaron was practicing piano in the living room; he was ten years old and wanted to be Arthur Rubinstein, but he had no talent. We all went into the kitchen in our pajamas and robes. My mother cautioned us not to eat too much cereal because this was Thanksgiving Day and there'd be turkey and all the trimmings at Grandma Rozalia's.

"Which reminds me," she said, and picked up the phone. We were still living on Columbus Avenue, and there was a phone hanging over the kitchen counter. My mother stood at the counter in her apron, dialing Grandma Rozalia's number.

I could hear only my mother's end of the conversation. From what I could gather, Grandma was telling her there'd been some sort of mistake. She'd thought we were going to Grandma *Kate's* for Thanksgiving. My mother said, "Mama, how can we be going to Kate's? Terry abandoned us, we don't go to Kate's anymore, are you getting senile?" My mother listened. So did all us kids. "No, Mama," she said, "we made these plans a long time ago, don't you remember? Anyway, it's academic, isn't it? Academic. Well, I'm sorry you don't know what that means, Mama, but it's a word. 'Academic.' It means Terry and I are separated, Terry and I are getting a divorce, we can't go to his mother's on Thanksgiving Day." She listened a moment and then said, "Mama, I *know* we usually come to you on *Passover,* but things are different now, and besides, Mama, you *invited* us!" She listened again, and then said, "I don't know when." Pause. "September." Another pause. "October maybe, I know you invited us. Things have been so crazy around here . . ." She listened again. "So what are you saying? We're *not* invited there today? Is that what you're saying?" And listened again. "Let me get this straight, Mama. There's no *room* at the table? Is that what you're saying? *Who?*" She listened and said, "They're not even *family.* There's room at your Thanksgiving Day table for *strangers,* but there's no room for your daughter and your three grandchildren, is *that* what you're saying?" She listened and said, "Then what *are* you saying, Mama?" And listened. And said, "I see. Uh-huh." And listened again. "The big table seats ten, uh-huh, and you've already got twelve at it, and you're putting the kids at the smaller round table off the foyer, I see. So it looks like all your other children will be there having turkey with you and some *strangers* because you haven't got room for *us!*" And listened for just an instant, and then said, "No, you listen to *me,* Mama!" and stopped listening altogether. "If there's no room for us, then we're not coming, we wouldn't *dream* of inconveniencing you. But let me tell you, Mama, you're not going to see us in that house ever again. So give all our love, don't interrupt me, Mama, to all your fortunate children who'll be there with you today, but don't hold your breath till you see *us* again!" and slammed down the phone.

"What'd you *do?*" Aaron asked.

"What'd *I* do? What'd your *grandmother* do, no room at the table!"

"If there's no room, there's no room, Mom. What do you want her to do, build a bigger house?"

"Why'd she invite strangers?"

"Because she didn't know we were coming."

"I can understand family, but *strangers?* And then there's no room at the *table?* I'll never go there again, Aaron."

"Mom, don't be . . ."

"And *you're* never going there again, either," she told all of us. "We were invited a *month* ago! *Two* months ago! You know what she accomplished today? She kissed this family goodbye, is what she accomplished. Her own daughter, her grandchildren, she kissed us all goodbye."

"Is everybody disappearing?" Annie asked.

In January, Grandma came over in the middle of the night to tell my mother she had cancer.

They made up after that.

❑

We sit on the sofa in the vast empty living room, sipping coffee, my mother and I. It is now five-thirty in the morning. Morngloam has not yet begun to tint the eastern sky. The night is still black out there, and Annie has been gone for almost four hours. We do not know what to say to each other. It seems to me that my mother and I have not known what to say to each other for the longest time now, perhaps ever since my father went away. She sips her coffee the way Grandma Rozalia used to, pinky extended in the European manner, as if she is holding a demitasse instead of a breakfast cup. Her eyes are hollow. I hate what my sister does to her.

"Do you think there might be something in her letters?" she asks.

"What letters? She didn't leave a letter, did she?"

"No, I mean the ones she sent me over the years."

"I doubt it. Why would there be anything in her letters?"

"Places she went, things she did. Maybe she's going back to one of them. I don't know."

She sighs heavily. The sigh is one of utter despair.

"Do you have them?" I ask.

"Shall I get them?" she asks, and without waiting for an answer, she rises and walks softly into the bedroom. I sit alone in the living room. The house seems so empty and still. My mother returns with a tiny rubber-banded packet of envelopes in her hand. She sits beside me, and hands the packet to me. I remove the rubber band, slip it over my wrist. The first letter reads:

Dear Mom:

Thanks for the idea for the Fourth of July, but I'm not sure I want to go to the Embassy to mingle with a lot of Americans. Anyway, I've been meeting plenty of Americans here in Amsterdam, and they are a lot of fun, but only for a short while. I have finally rented a studio where I can work. It is a 30 minute walk to the center, next to a beautiful park and shopping area. The studio actually is an old school house that has very long corridors, a shower, toilets, washing machine, garden. My part of the studio used to be the gymnasium, so there are still painted stripes and circles that were used for the basketball courts. It's huge with really big windows all around.

I share the studio with another artist, my age, who used to be a translator for the UN, who is married with two kids. She is quite successful and is able to make a living from her large watercolors that are both figurative and colorful. She is rarely there, so I have a peaceful place to work. The rent is also very cheap. There are many tables so I have spread out my jewelry and my sketches for future pieces and am embarking on some new avenues of exploration. Cool. I will try to call you sometime soon. Hope all is well with you. All my love, Annie.

There is no return address on the envelope.

It occurs to me that in all of her journeys, my sister never gave us the names of people she was living with or renting from or traveling with. She would not even give us the name of a hotel or a B&B where she was staying only temporarily. If pressed on the telephone, she would say, "I don't know the name." If you told her that everybody in the world knows the name of the hotel he's staying at, she would say, "This is just a small hotel, I don't know the name." If you told her to go talk to the manager and ask him the name of the hotel, she'd say, "I'll do that to-morrow," and then she wouldn't call for the next month, by which time she would have changed hotels, and would claim she didn't know the name of the new one.

There is no return address on the second envelope, either. I take the letter from it, unfold it, and begin reading:

Dear Mom:

Well, I've moved out of the big studio and am now living in the back of a little shop. There's no shower, just a small sink in the toilet, but I can't tell you how good it feels to be on my own after sharing a studio with a woman who went through my bags every night and scattered broken glass around my bed! I am making . . .

"Did *what?*"
"Where are you?"
"Here. The broken glass."
"I have no idea."

. . . I am making some quite beautiful pieces and am ex-hibiting them in the window, but so far no one has expressed any interest in purchasing them, although they appear to definitely get people's interest as they stroll by. I hope you had a wonderful holiday, full of Love and Joy. I will be in Amsterdam for another month at least, depending on how the shop goes, but I have to tell you some very strange people have been wandering by, including a couple of skinheads who made threatening gestures. Thanks for the birthday money. Will call soon. Much love, Annie.

"What's this about skinheads?"
"I wouldn't be surprised."

"What do you mean? Some guys *threatening* her?"

"Her jewelry can be very provocative. Well, you know her jewelry."

The stamp on the next envelope is most certainly from Indonesia, but again, there is no return address. The letter itself is very short:

Dear Mom:

I have been living in the ruins of an old temple. There is no electricity, but behind the temple is a long valley and a fresh water spring. One day a pink flamingo came to the valley and waded in the sea for an hour and then flew away. I love you and miss you. Annie.

"Are there flamingos in Indonesia?"

"If there are flamingos in Miami, there are flamingos in Indonesia. What are you thinking? That she was seeing things?"

The next letter is on lined paper torn from a spiral notebook. It reads:

Sunday

Dear Mom:

After our rather animated telephone conversation yesterday, I have decided that for your benefit I will consider accepting catastrophic health insurance. There are two conditions which must be met before I enter into such a contract. First of all the insurance would only be for medical and not for psychiatric. Secondly, I would have complete control over the choice of treatment and the power to refuse any recommendations from any doctors.

I know you are . . .

"When was this?" I ask. "Where was she?"

"Greece, I think. I'm not sure."

"Which trip?"

"Look at the envelope. There should be a date on the envelope."

I turn the envelope over in my hands. The stamp and postmark are indeed Greek, but the date is illegible.

I know you are very concerned that if I have a severe medical condition, you will be thrust into a situation where you can lose your financial security. Because I have great love and compassion for you, I want you to have peace of mind.

"What severe medical condition were you worried about, Mom?"

"A young girl traveling alone, all over the world, who knew what might happen?"

"But Annie smelled *mental* condition, didn't she?"

"I don't know what she smelled or didn't smell. I was only concerned that she have proper medical care if ever she needed it."

Please look into this for me and see if my conditions can be achieved. I've enclosed a little sketch of a pin I hope to make as soon as I can find a place to work. Please accept it as a Mother's Day gift. Thanks. Annie.

"Did you ever get that insurance for her?"

"I tried. Her conditions were impossible to meet."

There was a postcard showing a lagoon and a white sand beach identified as Koh Tao, Thailand. The postmark on the Thai stamp was Ko Phangan. Annie had written:

Dear Mom:

Have been enjoying life here and am healthy and fit. Meeting many different kinds of people from all over the world. Many laughs. Traveling alone makes one open your heart to everyone because you just have to feel Love. Hope you are well. Love, Annie.

And lastly, there was a long undated letter that started with the words *Happy Birthday, Mom!*, so it had to've been written in April sometime because that's when my mother's birthday is:

Happy birthday, Mom!

Tong Nai Pam is a large bay surrounded by dense jungle mountains. Two long white coral beaches separated by a tuft of peninsula and more mountain. A small path up the mountain and through the forest connects the two facing beaches.

The route takes about 15 minutes of walking time as it wangles its way here and there around large boulders, hanging vines, and crisp oval leaves, dried and layered on the jungle floor. It is quiet and peaceful here. An occasional rustle of lizard, the silent holes of some invisible unknown predator. I wonder what lives in those arm-sized holes, and whether they are sleeping or thinking about me thumping through their peaceful ageless gardens.

It is always a life and death walk for me. I have made it maybe 10 times now, each time alone, and each time knowing that if I am bitten by a King Cobra, I will end up fertilizer for some wayward palm before anyone either hears my fuzzy pleas for help or I crawl, poisoned, to my imminent demise.

A 15 minute death walk on a daily basis gets the blood flowing, pops the eyes open and wide. Feeling every root and vine with all my being, but just for the briefest of moments, before shifting to the next form, breathlessly anticipating movement. I have never seen a King Cobra on this path, but I swear I can hear them dreaming.

"Did you read this letter?" I ask.

"Of course, I read it. I read all her letters. There weren't that many, you know."

"What'd you think, Mom?"

"I thought she wrote very well. For someone who never went to college."

" 'Shifting to the next *form*'? What does that mean?"

"She probably meant 'shifting to the next *foot*.' She's walking through a forest, you know. Feeling every root and vine underfoot."

"Shifting to the next form," I say again, repeating the words as if this will help me understand them.

"A slip of the pen," my mother says.

"Mm."

"Why? What do you think, Professor? She's Dracula changing into a bat?"

"Cobras dreaming," I say. "She heard cobras dreaming."

"That was simile," she says, and shrugs.

I look at her.

"You know what simile is, don't you, Professor?"

"Sure. It's the same thing as metaphor."

I point my finger at her like a pistol, pull the imaginary trigger.

"Gotcha," I say.

Mama doesn't even smile.

I slip the rubber band from my wrist and onto the envelopes again. I am thinking it is such a slender body of correspondence for so many mighty journeys. I hand the bundle back to her. Mama places it on her lap, sighs at it, as if it has let her down somehow.

"Maybe we should call that woman, after all," she says.

For a moment, I'm not sure who she means.

"Woman?" I say.

"The shrink you saw last week."

"Oh."

"Whatever her name was. Was she any good, Andrew?"

"Lang. Yes, she seemed okay."

"Only okay?"

"She seemed fine, Mom."

"Did Annie mention what they talked about?"

"I was there, Mom. I know what they talked about."

"What do you mean, you were there? You mean in the *room* with them?"

"Yes, Mom. Annie wanted me to come in."

"And she *let* you? The shrink?"

"Her name is Lang, Mom, Dr. Lang. She's a respected psychiatrist at Mount . . ."

"And she let you *hear* what a patient was saying?"

"I told you, Annie wanted me to come in."

"That's highly unusual, isn't it?"

"I don't know if it's unusual or not."

"Well, it seems *highly* unusual to me."

"So be it."

"What's that supposed to mean, so be it?"

"It means if you think it was unusual, then you think it was unusual. Apparently, Dr. Lang didn't think it was so unusual because she permitted it."

My mother nods.

Her nods mean either "You are a jackass, son," or "There's no use even talking to you." In this instance, her nod probably means both.

"So what'd your sister tell her?"

"She said she was molested when she was a kid."

"Nonsense."

"When she was eleven years old."

"No."

"She said Mr. Alvarez put his hand under her skirt . . ."

"Who on earth is Mr . . . Oh. The *super?* When we were living on Seventy-second Street? Annie never said any such thing! You're making this up."

"Stuck his finger in her, she says. She wet her pants. She peed on his hand."

"Really, Andrew."

"Mother, it's what she told Dr. Lang."

"Dr. *Lang!*" she says.

"She also said she heard Mr. Alvarez's voice coming from the television set."

"Well," my mother says. "Everyone hears voices."

"What does that mean?"

"I'm sure Annie didn't mean actually hearing *his* voice coming from the television. Or maybe she was just listening to thoughts inside her head. Everyone has internal thoughts, Andrew. You teach English, haven't you ever heard of interior monologues?"

"Yes, Mother, I . . ."

"*Ulysses*, remember, Professor? *Finnegans Wake?*"

"I'm merely repeating what Annie . . ."

"Or didn't you ever study James Joyce?"

Her sarcasm is biting. I am suddenly five years old again. My father is gone. He never answered my letter. I have no father. I keep crying all the time. My mother keeps telling me to stop crying all the time, I can't seem to stop crying. Aaron rabbit-punches me every time he passes me in the apartment. The apartment seems so huge with my father gone. Whenever I start crying, Annie begins crying, too. We are a gang, my sister and I.

My mother is pacing now.

"What else did Annie tell this Lang woman?" she asks.

This Lang Woman. Some sort of devious mid-Victorian figure with high hair and a corseted waist and a plumed hat, stalking drawing rooms and salons where she smiles secretly and eavesdrops on the confidences of young Tantric initiates. With those three words, my mother washes down the drain four years of college and four years of medical school and four years of psychiatric residency, leaving "This *Lang* Woman" standing exposed for the charlatan and quack she most certainly is.

"She told her all about Sicily."

"*All* about Sicily?"

"Well, almost everything, Mother."

"Told her what that doctor . . ."

"Said they all thought she was crazy, yes."

She whirls on me suddenly. Her eyes are blazing the way they had that night long ago, when she called my sister a little pisspants. I expect another bowl of mashed potatoes on my head. I almost cower from her.

"And you let her *say* all this?"

"Mom, it was her nickel."

"*Her* nickel? *My* nickel, you mean, don't you?"

"Annie was *there* to talk. What good would it have done if . . ."

"What were you *thinking?*" she yells. "Did you suddenly lose your . . . ?"

She cuts herself short. I suspect she was about to suggest that perhaps I'd suddenly lost *my* mind, too, but of course this observation would have been at odds with what she believes, or disbelieves, to be the truth about Annie. She begins pacing again, stalking the room like a lynx, all green-eyed and auburn-haired with a little help from a rinse bottled by my brother's firm. I cannot tell whether she is furious or merely desperate.

"Mom," I say, "she's gone again, okay?"

My mother nods.

"Let's just try to find her, okay?"

She nods again.

"Mom?"

She keeps nodding. I can't even imagine what's going on inside her head. She just keeps pacing silently, nodding.

"Okay, Mom?"

"Yes," she says at last. "Okay."

And nods again.

4

My father used to smoke incessantly.

I loved to watch him paint.

I have seen many movies about painters, some famous, some striving to become famous, and none of them have ever seemed convincing to me. When my father painted, there was nothing but him and the canvas. He was utterly alone with the canvas. I would come home from school and walk into the spare bedroom of our apartment, on the north side, where the light was good, and he would be standing at the easel wearing jeans and sandals and a blue smock like the ones French street cleaners wear, and which I think he actually bought in Paris, I know he had dozens of them, all of them paint-spattered. The smocks themselves looked like one of his canvases.

We were still living in the building on Seventy-second Street at the time—yes, the one where Mr. Alvarez was super—and he would always ask me when I came home from school, "Is your father still painting?" and I would say, "Yes, he is, Mr. Alvarez," because what else would my father be doing but painting? I sometimes thought he painted day and night. I sometimes thought he never slept. All he did was paint and smoke his little Brazilian cigars, which he called in a thick fake Spanish accent, "gringo steenkers," blowing out clouds of smoke and grinning like one of the banditos in *Treasure of the Sierra Madre*. He was never without one of those little cigars in his mouth. Never. He would lean in close to the canvas, as if scrutinizing each dollop of paint he applied with putty knife or brush or even thumb, squinting at every new stroke, puffing on the cigar, backing away, dipping into the riot of color on the enamel tray he used as a palette, lunging at the canvas again, puffing, painting. I loved to watch him paint.

He was a large man, my father—I talk about him as if he's dead, when I know he's not—and he overwhelmed the easel and the canvas and the tiny room in which he was permitted to work. But even later, when he was recognized and rich and had built for himself the huge studio in Connecticut, he triumphed over this larger space with the sheer bulk of his size and the energy of his attack upon each oversized canvas. He always painted big. Fair-haired and pale-eyed, he slashed at the canvas like a Viking invader hacking a hapless black-Irish peasant to bits, trailing a wide red gash here, exploding a burst of white there, dipping his thumb into burnt umber or cobalt blue, poking it at the canvas as if gouging out an eye. The flaxen hair and blue eyes in fact bespoke of fierce Norwegian ancestry, not for nothing had Norsemen once sailed up the river Shannon. The gentleness of his spirit murmured of something quite else. Soft green hills and drifting mist. Smooth brown whiskey. A lullaby on a moonless night. A keening graveside woman. My father's soul was Irish to the core.

When he read to us at night . . .

I have to tell you, first, that he loved to play board games with us. Along around five-thirty or six each evening, he would come out of his studio (he called even the tiny back room a "studio"), stinking of cigar smoke and turpentine, and even before my mother called us to dinner he would say, "Hey, kiddos, some Monopoly after supper?" (He still called dinner "supper," the way Grandma Kate always did.) Or Risk, which was another game. Or Clue. My mother would always tell us to finish our homework first, but every night, nonetheless, we would sit down to play a board game for an hour or so after dinner.

My sister didn't like playing board games. "Are you bored, darlin?" my father would ask her. (He was an inveterate punster, which my mother said was his way of taking revenge on the English language, the same way she maintains sarcasm is her way of doing it.) Annie was indeed bored, and a punster in her own right. "No, Dad, just *Terry*-fied of losing," she would say, making a pun on my father's name, which Aaron never seemed to get even though it had become a standard response to my father's board/bored question. A fiercely competitive player, Aaron was too busy concentrating on the game itself, whichever game it happened to be. Whenever he was losing, he would knock the board and all its pieces off the table. "*Oop*-a-la!" my father would shout, and burst out laughing, but my mother would send Aaron to his room, anyway.

At night, after we had carefully put whichever game away, its pieces still in position for the next night's foray, we would go into the room Aaron and I shared, which was larger than Annie's, and we would curl up on one of the beds, and my father would read to us. He read all sorts of bedtime stories to us, but his favorite—and ours as well—was *The Once and Future King*. Even Aaron liked this one, though I think at first he identified with Kay, "who was too dignified to have a nickname" and who would be called Sir Kay when he grew older. Aaron didn't know, of course, that the Wart would grow up to be King Arthur.

There were four volumes in the book, but my father read only the first one to us, and so we didn't learn anything about the interlocking Arthurian tales of incest and infidelity. Neither did any of us have the slightest inkling that at this exact moment in time our father was "playing around," as my mother later explained it to us, and might therefore have had an affinity for the Guinevere-Lancelot parts of the story, if ever he'd got around to reading those to us, which he never did. What interested us about *The Sword in the Stone,* as this first volume was called, was not T. H. White's concern with *force majeure* (which we wouldn't have recognized if it came up behind us and hit us on the head with a club) but instead the way he and Merlin together worked their magic.

Aaron was eight years old in that year before my father abandoned us. Annie and I were each four. In the soft light from the lamp beside Aaron's bed, we listened to my father's liquid voice as he began reading to us yet another time, crediting the book and its author each and every night before continuing with the story—"This is *The Once and Future King,* by T. H. White"—and then conjuring for us the twelfth-century England White had created.

Spellbound, we listened.

> *She is not any common earth*
> *Water or wood or air,*
> *But Merlin's Isle of Gramarye*
> *Where you and I shall fare*

This was the opening epigraph of the first volume, and my father read it with portentous intonations proper to the magical proceedings that would follow.

"Who's Grandma Marie?" Annie asked.

"It's *Gram*-a-ree," my father said. "It's White's name for England. It also means magic."

"Who's Merlin?" Aaron asked.

"A magician," my father said. "Are you going to listen to this, or shall we just turn out the lights and go to bed?"

"What does 'Where you and I shall fare' mean?" I asked.

"In a minute, it's going to mean fare thee well."

"What's fare thee well?" Annie asked.

"It's good night, Toots," my father said.

"Is Toots a pun?" Annie asked.

❑

The minute Daddy got famous, he bought a house in Connecticut. Paintings that were earlier selling for $3,000 a week before were this week selling for $100,000, and a week after that for $300,000. At great cost, he transformed some old stables on the property into a spacious studio with terrific skylights, where he could smoke his smelly little Brazilian cigars while he painted all day long and sometimes deep into the night. (I always thought he and Grandma Rozalia smelled exactly alike with their tobacco stink. Except Daddy had a turpentine smell besides.)

My mother got not only the house in the divorce settlement, but also the studio and everything in it. This came to quite a bit of change; when she locked him out of her house and her life, there were paintings valued at two-million-five stacked in the old carriage house. She promptly sold all the paintings ("Good riddance to bad rubbish!" she announced) and moved all of us back full-time to the apartment we still kept in New York. But at first, we continued to use the house during the summer months. And one summer, when Aaron was fourteen, and my sister and I were ten, someone broke into the house one night.

We didn't know this had happened until the next morning, when we were all sitting down to breakfast and Aaron was going out to get the *New York Times* from the mailbox, and he noticed that one of the glass panels on the back door to the house, the kitchen door, was smashed. My mother suspected at once that it was my "no-good father," as she called him, even though all evidence had him living in San Miguel de Allende with an Irish girl who was purportedly his new model and mistress. I later saw one of the paintings he'd done of her during that time in his life. Actually, I went looking for it in MOMA's permanent collection. Even given my father's abstractionist bent, *Molly O* (the name of the painting *and* the girl) was identifiably redheaded, green-eyed, and blessed with three abundant breasts, surely hyperbole.

My mother called Mr. Schneider, the contractor who had renovated the stables when we first bought the house. A portly little man with a heavy German accent, he kept telling my mother she should keep up with house repairs, that it was a "zad t'ing" (I can't do accents) to see a fine old house "like zis one" fall into neglect. She always pooh-poohed his concern. I don't think she'd even have had the glass panel replaced if its absence wasn't letting in bugs at night. Mr. Schneider came over with a glazier the next day, and stood with his hands on his hips, watching the man as he replaced the glass panel, clucking his tongue every now and then, perhaps thinking something like this would never have happened in his native Germany.

Two nights later, someone broke into the house again.

This time, a different panel on the back door was broken.

We figured that whoever was trespassing had broken the glass so he could reach in and turn the simple spring latch on the door. The odd thing was that nothing was missing from the house, and no one had heard anyone coming in or going out. The bedroom my mother used to share with my father was on the second floor of the house, at the end opposite the ground floor kitchen. Besides, she was a sound sleeper, so it wasn't surprising that she hadn't heard anything. Annie slept right down the hall from her, in a room just over the kitchen. If anyone could have heard the intruder, it was Annie. But she claimed she had heard nothing. Aaron and I shared a room on the third floor of the house, in what used to be the attic. Neither of us had heard any sound of glass breaking, or doors opening, or anything of the sort, but after the third nocturnal visit, we both started listening very hard. That was the last break-in, though, the third one. Mr. Schneider brought his glazier over after each time, and stood by with his hands on his hips, clucking his tongue, while the glass panel was fixed.

My mother called the police after the third visit, but they were a Mickey Mouse department and they didn't take fingerprints or any-thing, and besides it never happened again, so that was the end of that. My mother never surrendered her belief that my father had been break-ing into the house out of Irish spite. Aaron and I figured a squirrel or a raccoon had been breaking the glass on the kitchen door, trying to get at the food in the pantry. Only Annie knew it wasn't any squirrel or rac-coon breaking that glass.

She told me years later that she used to sneak out of the house in her nightgown, and run down the hill through the trees, past Daddy's studio to where the property joined the main road. There she would lie on her belly in the dark, watching automobiles speed by in the dead of night. Sometimes, when she got back to the house, she found the kitchen door locked behind her. She would break the glass panel just above the lock, and then reach in to open the door. Once she cut her hand. When she mentioned all this, I asked her why she would do such a thing. Leave the house in the middle of the night to go watch cars speeding by on the road below. She told me she thought Daddy might be coming back. She told me she was waiting for Daddy.

Now I wonder if my father was the start of it all.

Her neurosis, or whatever it is.

Whatever has caused her to run away again in the middle of the night.

❑

In the summer of 1982, my mother took Annie and me to Europe. We visited Denmark and Sweden and Norway, the Scandinavian Tour, except that we never got to Finland because my mother said it was too close to Russia and this was still during the Cold War, and she was afraid there'd be a pogrom or something. It was in Stockholm, at our hotel, that my sister fell in love with an eighteen-year-old waiter named Sven. She was fifteen at the time. Our birthdays are in September, and this was in August.

"Oh, he's so *beautiful*," she used to tell me, which I guess he was, with my sister's blond hair and green eyes, almost a third twin except that he was much taller than I, and spoke English with a marked accent. We were moving on to Norway the following week. My sister stared at Sven goggle-eyed and open-mouthed while he brought us double desserts. My mother thought it was cute, Annie being so smitten and all. I thought it was dangerous. I knew what eighteen-year-old boys wanted from beautiful young girls. Especially eighteen-year-old *Swedish* boys. When he asked her to go for a walk one night, my mother said Sure, why not, what's the harm?

I followed them at a discreet distance. Well, not too discreet. I didn't want to lose them. I didn't want him working his Swedish charms on my unsuspecting little sister, my kid sister. I am five minutes older than she is. I chipped my collar bone coming out of my mother's womb, preparing the way for both of us. They had to put me in an incubator. When the doctor came in to report this to my mother, he said, "One of your twins, the boy, is a little rocky, so we put him in an incubator." A little *rocky!* His exact words. My mother almost expired on the spot. He was trying to tell her I'd experienced some discomfort breaking my collar bone. Anyway, he walked her by the lake, young Sven did. My fifteen-year-old sister. He kissed her by the lake. I wanted to strangle him. I kept watching. One false move . . .

But no, that was it.

That solitary kiss by the lake, under a full moon. And then he walked her back to the hotel, and . . . well, wait a minute . . . he kissed her once again. I watched her go up the steps into the hotel. I watched him looking after her as she disappeared. Then he put his hands in his pockets and walked away.

She sent him postcards every day.

It was as if my mother and I were no longer with her. All through Norway, she talked of him day and night. We'd be having lunch or dinner, she'd be scribbling postcards to him, sometimes three or four postcards a day. It was infuriating. And humiliating. We were invisible. His birthday was at the end of August, she wanted to send him a gift. We went shopping all one day, looking for an appropriate shirt for him. She made me try on six or seven shirts she liked, to see how they looked. I told her Sven was bigger than I was. She said, "That's okay, I just want to get an idea." Six or seven shirts. Maybe eight. She finally picked a lime-green, short-sleeved shirt she said would go well with his blond hair and green eyes. My mother thought all of this was cute, even though she was the one who paid for the shirt. In retrospect, this is not strange. She's been paying for my sister's voyage through life ever since.

We got back home at the beginning of September. There was no communication from Sven, not a letter, not a postcard, nothing. No acknowledgment that he had received any of her ten thousand postcards, no thank you for the lime-green birthday shirt, nothing. Our own birthday was on the eighteenth. My mother planned to throw a sweet-sixteen party for us. Annie and I insisted that we supply the music.

Our group was called The Boppers, which was a play on the expression "teeny-boppers" and a reference as well to the time-honored series of books about The Bobbsey Twins, not to mention a sidelong wink at "bop," which was very far from the kind of music we were playing at the time. This was 1982, remember. The Beatles had broken up long ago. In fact, John Lennon had been killed almost two years ago. Paul McCartney had recorded a song called "Ebony and Ivory" with Stevie Wonder, and it was now the number-four song on the charts. The Boppers imitated it to perfection. We also played "Eye of the Tiger," the Survivor hit, and "Don't You Want Me" from the Human League, and we did a fair rendition of the Steve Miller Band's "Abracadabra," too. Not to mention all the Golden Oldies from when you and I were young, Gertie. Altogether, we weren't a bad band.

I played bass guitar, and my sister played the tambourines and sang. She had a strong, clear voice, not unlike Janis Joplin's, or so everyone, including me, told her. We used to rehearse in a church hall six blocks from the apartment we were still living in with my mother; Aaron was already off at college. We kept all our equipment at the church . . . well, not my guitar. But everything else. Tuners and amplifiers and speakers, and microphones, all the stuff every garage band in the nation, or perhaps the world, had to buy if they ever hoped to achieve instant stardom. My mother had paid for the equipment, of course. It had cost something like six thousand dollars.

Two days before our birthday, after we'd been rehearsing for close to ten days, my sister hocked all the equipment, bought herself a ticket to Stockholm, and ran off to meet her beloved Sven. Of course, we didn't know where she'd gone at first. We just knew she was gone. Aaron was the one who suggested that she'd gone in search of her "inamorato," the exact word he used. This was confirmed at the beginning of October, when we received a postcard from an island called Visby. It read, "Can't find Sven, moving on, love to you all. Annie." Not even a happy birthday to me.

Not even that.

In retrospect, though, her search through the Scandinavian countries, and later London and Paris, was the shortest of all her excursions. She was still a minor at the time, and after my mother contacted the State Department, they were able to track her comings and goings through various ports of entry and finally located her in a seedy hotel on the Left Bank.

When my mother got her on the phone, she told her that unless she was on the next plane to New York, she would have the French police arrest her, a threat Annie apparently believed because, lo and behold, she showed up at the apartment two days later, looking none the worse for wear, and telling us smugly that there were far better-looking men than Sven Lindqvist in this wide world of ours. We thought she was cured of her adolescent crush as well as her recent wanderlust.

But after what happened in Sicily, I wonder if Annie accepted my mother's threat of arrest only because the FBI had already entered the landscape of her mind.

❑

"The New Year's Eve Incident," as the family later referred to it, took place in December of 1983, a bit more than three months after our seventeenth birthday. By then, I was going steady with a girl named Rosemary Quinn who was sixteen and a junior at Ambrose. Annie, being mean, said Rosemary probably still wore white cotton panties. She also said she probably didn't know how to kiss, a misapprehension I didn't bother to correct. I was taking Rosemary to a party on West

Seventy-ninth Street that night. A twenty-one-year-old boy who was a senior at Dartmouth picked up Annie at nine o'clock and took her to a party in Greenwich Village. My mother, at the age of forty-one, had begun dating a bald lawyer who was fifty-four years old and who lived in a white clapboard house overlooking a pond. She went to a party at his house in Larchmont, New York.

My mother and I were both home by four A.M.

Annie still wasn't home by the time the sun came up.

Neither of us was particularly alarmed.

I made scrambled eggs (which were a bit runny, my mother kindly informed me) and she and I sat in the kitchen drinking coffee and eating and watching the sun come up over Manhattan. She told me Douglas Feingold was really a very nice man, but that she couldn't see herself getting sexually involved with him (thank you for sharing that, Mom) and then she went into her "My Son the Doctor" routine (although Aaron was in Business Administration and not Pre-Med), kvelling about how well he was doing at Princeton where he would be starting his last semester next year (and incidentally meeting the future Mrs. Gulliver, young Gussie Manners serving up burgers at Ye Olde Mickey D's). As I say, this was 1983—well, 1984 already—and the cotton was high, and neither of us even thought to wonder about where the hell Annie might be until it occurred to me that it was almost nine A.M. on the first day of the new year, and no sign of her, and she hadn't even called to say good morning and happy new year.

I asked my mother if she knew where Annie had been headed for with the twenty-one-year-old Dartmouth senior, and she said Annie had left a number . . .

"Which I've always insisted on," she said.

. . . and she went fishing in the drawer under the wall telephone and found a slip of paper with the name Josh Levine scribbled on it, and a telephone number under that.

"Is this the Dartmouth guy's name?" I asked. "Or the name of the guy where the party was?"

"The Dartmouth guy is a Wasp named Freddie Cole," my mother said with some contempt, since she had always considered my father a Wasp even though he was a Catholic.

"Do you think Annie would be angry if we called her?"

"To wish her a happy new year?" my mother said.

"Well, to see if she's okay."

"Why wouldn't she be okay?"

"I don't know. It's already nine, five *after* nine, in fact," I said, looking at my watch again.

"Call her," my mother said. "She'll be happy to hear from us."

I dialed the number on the scrap of paper. The phone rang once, twice, three times . . .

"Hello?"

A girl's voice. At first I thought it was . . .

"Annie?"

"No, this is Irene."

"Irene, hi, this is Andy Gulliver. Is my sister still there?"

"Who's your sister?"

"Annie. She came there with . . . uh . . . Freddie Cole? Is he there?"

"Just a sec," Irene said.

I waited.

My mother looked at me.

I shrugged.

"Hello?"

A man's voice.

"Who's this?" I asked.

"Freddie Cole."

"Hi, Freddie, this is Annie's brother. Could I speak to her, please?"

There was a silence on the line.

"Freddie?"

"Yes?"

"Could I speak to my sister, please?"

"She's resting," Freddie said.

"Well . . . uh . . . could you get her, please? I'd like to talk to her."

"Okay," Freddie said.

He put the phone down, I heard it clattering on the table top or the counter or whatever. I heard voices, laughter, more voices. My mother looked at me again.

"He's getting her," I said.

"Where is she?"

"Resting."

"What do you mean? You mean sleeping?"

"He said resting."

"Who did?"

"Freddie."

We kept waiting. I looked at my watch. It was ten minutes past nine. "Freddie?" I said into the phone, hoping he would hear my voice and pick up the receiver again. No one picked up. "Freddie!" I shouted into the phone. Nothing. No one. I whistled into the phone. I whistled louder. I could still hear voices and laughter in the background.

"Where is she?" my mother asked.

"I don't know, Mom."

She was already wearing a look I would come to know only too well in later years. A tight little mouth, a frown creasing her brow, puzzlement and suspicion in the green eyes, helplessness beginning to border on panic.

"Hello?"

"Annie?" I said.

Her voice sounded frail, distant, trancelike.

"Annie? Is that you?"

"Andy?"

"Yes, honey, what's the matter?"

"Did Sven call yet?" she asked, and a chill went up my spine.

"What is it?" my mother asked.

"Annie," I said, "where are you?"

In a voice that was lilting, almost sing-song, she said, "I don't know, where am I? Has Sven called yet?"

"Annie, put Freddie on the line, okay?"

"Freddie?"

"The boy who took you to the party."

"Freddie?"

"Freddie Cole. Please get him, Annie. And stay near the phone. Don't go away, all right?"

"How can I get Freddie if I don't leave the phone?" she asked, and began giggling.

"Just go get him, okay? Hurry, Annie!"

"Oh, okay," she said in the same sing-song voice, and I heard the phone clattering down again.

"Andrew, what *is* it?" my mother said.

"I don't know."

"You were *speaking* to her, what do you mean you don't . . . ?"

"I'm trying to find out, Mom."

"Where is she now?"

"She went to get him."

"Let me talk to him."

"He's not here yet, Mom."

"Well, *where* is he? Why'd you let her get off the phone? What the hell is . . . ?"

"Hello?"

"Freddie?"

"Yes."

"What's wrong with my sister?"

"Nothing. Why? What's wrong with her?"

"Is she drunk?"

"How do I know what she is?"

"Look, you son of a bitch . . ."

"Hey! *Hey!* Don't you go . . ."

"Where are you? Where's that party you're at?"

"What is it?" my mother said.

"Just don't go calling . . ."

"Give me the address there."

"I don't *know* the fucking address."

"Get it! And fast!"

"What *is* it?" my mother said again.

❑

In the taxi, I repeated every word of the conversation I'd had with Annie on the phone, and my mother kept saying over and over again, "It's dope, they doped her." I didn't know if it was dope or not. I was seventeen and I had never so much as smoked a joint. I'm now thirty-six, and I admit to having smoked marijuana since, but only several times in my life, and then only because I didn't want to seem like a spoil sport. When you're in college, and everybody around you is smoking, you don't want the girls to think you're a wuss.

This was New Year's Day, and there wasn't any traffic at all in the streets. In fact, I think we were lucky even to find a cab. We made it down to Tenth Street in something like twelve minutes. The cabbie let us out in front of a brownstone in a row of similar buildings. I tipped him three dollars on an eight-dollar ride, and he wished us a happy new year and drove off. My mother looked suddenly old and frail. This was the second time I'd seen her look that way. The first was when Annie sold the band equipment and went flying off to Europe. In later years, this look would become commonplace. I realize now that Annie's frequent disappearances made all of us look old before our time.

The guy who answered the door said he was Josh Levine. I figured him to be twenty-three or -four, a good-looking guy with curly black hair and brown eyes, wearing a white shirt with the sleeves rolled up and the collar open, a red tie hanging loose on his chest. He said he was sorry for the way Freddie had behaved on the telephone, and he assured us that there was nothing to worry about, Annie had just consumed a little too much alcohol. "Consumed" was the exact word he used. (I later learned he had gone to Harvard. He told me that while we were waiting for the doctor.)

Freddie himself was nowhere in sight, God knew where the little prick had run off to. My mother looked around the place disapprovingly. There were ashtrays brimming with butts, many of which I recognized as roaches, and there was the sweetish smell of marijuana on the air—which I don't think my mother detected as such—and there were girls and boys and women and men asleep on sofas or on strewn pillows all over the floor, and there were empty booze bottles and beer bottles, and a record player going with Michael Jackson's "Billie Jean." In the kitchen, a redheaded guy in his late forties, I guessed, was in very deep conversation with a girl who looked nineteen.

My sister was lying on her belly on a bed in a bedroom on the third floor of the building. She was still fully clothed, except for her shoes, but the back of her party dress was unzipped, and her bra clasp had been unfastened. I vowed at that moment that if I ever ran into Freddie Cole again, I would kill him. (I did, in fact, run into him five years later, at a singles bar in Brooklyn, when I was twenty-two and he was twenty-six. He was drunk, so I didn't kill him.) I sat on the edge of the bed. My mother stood at the foot, shaking her head. Her face was deathly white, her green eyes glistening with anger. Downstairs, far away, another record dropped into place. Men at Work doing "Down Under."

I shook my sister.

"Annie," I said, "wake up."

She rolled over. She tried to prop herself up, and then fell back against the pillow again.

"Annie," I said, "wake *up!*"

She opened her eyes. Tried to focus. Recognized me. Smiled.

"Oh, hello," she said. "Happy birthday."

❑

Dr. Aaron Tannenbaum had been our family doctor for as long as I could remember, but he wasn't too tickled to be making a house call on New Year's Day. He arrived at Josh Levine's brownstone at a quarter to eleven that morning. Cleanly shaved, impeccably tailored, he looked as if he might be going to brunch in the Palm Court instead of paying a visit to a stranger's apartment in the Village. Even the sight of two familiar faces—mine and my mother's—did nothing to mollify him. He greeted my mother gruffly—"Happy new year, Helene"—and then without so much as a hello to me, even though he'd been treating me for acne for the past four years, he asked where Annie was.

We took him up to the third-floor bedroom.

Annie was still out. Dr. Tannenbaum asked me to leave the room. I waited in the hallway outside while he examined her. When he and my mother joined me some ten minutes later, he sighed heavily and said, "I don't know what she's ingested, but whatever it was, it was a massive dose. Get her out of here, take her home, and put her to bed."

"Can't we pump out her stomach?" my mother asked.

"Wouldn't help a damn," Tannenbaum said. "Whatever it was has already been absorbed into her blood stream. Put her to bed. And pray to God she doesn't wake up a vegetable."

❑

Annie slept soundly for a bit more than thirty-six hours.

On the second of January in the year of our Lord 1984, she woke up, looked around her room, recognized my mother, recognized me, and in a very hoarse voice said, "Hi, what time is it?"

I told her it was eleven-thirty.

"Morning or night?" she asked.

"Night," I said.

"Want to watch Johnny Carson?" she said.

"Sure," I said.

"What'd you take?" my mother asked.

"Take?"

"Dr. Tannenbaum said you ingested a massive dose of some drug. What was it, Annie?"

"I have no idea, Mom."

"Annie, you were unconscious for . . ."

"Mom, leave her . . ."

"I was *not* un . . ."

"Don't tell *me* you have no idea what you *took!* You're lucky we didn't have your *stomach* pumped out!"

The room went silent.

"Somebody may have dropped something in my drink," Annie said.

"Why would anyone do that?"

"How should I know? People do crazy things," she said.

"What do you mean?"

"To get even."

"Get *even?* What are you talking about?"

"For being blond. And pretty. For having good breasts. Who the hell knows? People just *do* things. You have to watch yourself at all times. I'm hungry. Can I get something to eat?"

She wasn't a vegetable.

But we still didn't know what else she was.

❑

What happened to Annie in our senior year at Ambrose Academy was admittedly a bad break, no pun intended.

I find it difficult to think of my mother as a Soccer Mom, especially since the term did not exist back then in 1984. But assuredly, that's what she was. In March, you see, my sister had the good fortune—or bad, depending upon how you looked at it—to be elected co-captain of the soccer team, and it was in the fifth game of the season, as she was kicking the ball downfield toward the opposing team's goal, that Annie was blindsided by two girls in yellow and blue tunics and shorts, and knocked off her feet head over teacups, to land at a peculiar angle that broke her left leg.

In her hospital room, her leg in a cast and supported by pulleys and ropes, she told me, "They were after me, Andy. The were out to get me."

Actually, the girls who'd been responsible for the accident had come to the hospital only the day before, to apologize to Annie, and to tell my mother and me how sorry they were. I could not imagine that they'd been out to break Annie's leg deliberately. These were prep school girls. Even professional athletes wouldn't do anything so intentionally cruel. Would they?

"I'm telling you they were out to *get* me," Annie insisted. "I should have listened."

"What do you mean? Listened to who?"

"Haven't you ever *sensed* that something was about to happen? I should have listened to my own inner thoughts. But butter wouldn't melt in their mouths, you know?" she said, and here she fell into imitations of first the chunky redhead who was captain of the opposing team and next her slender blond co-captain, who in tandem had knocked Annie down. Annie's impressions were dead on, and actually quite funny, both girls shaking hands with her and wishing her luck before the game started, both of them being oh-so-sportsmanlike and rah-rah private-school ladies while secretly planning all along to hit her simultaneously at the thigh and the shin, ensuring a broken leg. "The two-faced bitches," Annie said.

"Annie, I'm sure they didn't . . ."

"Oh, *I'm* sure they *did*," she said, and handed me a Magic Marker and asked me to write something clever on her cast. I wrote "Give me a break, willya?" Annie thought it was funny.

She did not think the almost-two months she spent in a plaster cast to the hip was comical, however. Nor did she find even mildly amusing the additional six weeks she was forced to spend in a soft cast from her knee to her ankle. Riding the bus on crutches to and from school each day, she complained endlessly, becoming something of a kvetch who railed on about all the *mean* people in this world—"Like Blondie and her redheaded dyke girlfriend"—who couldn't bear seeing anyone else getting ahead in life.

Before the accident, she'd been a very good student. In fact, as I recall those days now, they form my happiest memories. Annie and I riding to school together on the bus, telling jokes and cracking wise with the other kids. Annie and I in class together, our hands popping up simultaneously whenever a teacher asked a question. My sister was the prettiest girl in the whole damn school, and I was her twin brother, and we were both smarter than anyone else around. We were The Gulliver Gang. My sister and I. We were twins.

But after her accident . . .

We thought it was the accident, you see.

We never once thought something might have happened to her in Sweden. Never once *imagined* anything had happened to her mind.

Even when she began losing interest in her classes, we blamed it on the accident. Now it was just *my* hand that popped up when a question was asked, my sister sitting unresponsive beside me. Or if, for example, a discussion was going on in class, where earlier Annie would have been a lively participant, she now sat silent and withdrawn. If a teacher asked, "Annie? Anything to contribute?" my sister would snap a surly "No!" or simply refuse to answer at all. Her concentration seemed to be fading. Sometimes, she didn't seem to be there at all. I told her she should stop thinking about the accident all the time, focus her energy instead on the future. This was our senior year at Ambrose. We both had college to look forward to.

I wasn't surprised when she started losing friends. At first, she just kept bad-mouthing the co-captains she insisted had deliberately broken her leg, but then she started accusing girls on the *Ambrose* team as well, her *own* team, suggesting that they'd also been part of the conspiracy somehow. Once, on my way to an English class, some girls from the team were whispering something as I approached, and all at once they stopped and turned away, and I figured they were talking about Annie, but I didn't know how to defend her because I myself thought her accusations were completely wrong-headed. Another time, I saw some girls openly mocking her, pretending to limp down the hall and yelling, "They broke my leg, they broke my leg!" and I went over and said, "Cut it out, it wasn't *you* who got hurt!"

Then my mother got a call after school one day, from the coach of the soccer team, who told her Annie was trying to work up a petition to get the two girls who'd broken her leg expelled from their school, and suggesting that Annie might want to schedule a talk with the psychiatrist at Ambrose. My mother took a fit. On the phone, she sounded the way she had that Thanksgiving morning when she was yelling at Grandma. "Are you suggesting there's something wrong with my daughter?" she said. "You try having *your* leg broken, see what effect it has on you! Her father abandoned her when she was five, you might take that into consideration as well. My daughter's an A-student, how *dare* you tell me she's crazy? Oh, no? Then what did you just say?" My mother listened and then said, "Yes, I *am* listening, how about *you* listening to me for a change? My daughter's not going to see any school psychiatrist! That's the end of that!" she shouted, and hung up.

For the next several days, my mother kept telling me she was going to have both of us transferred out of that school, did they think they were the only private school in New York, how *dared* they say such things about her daughter? I finally convinced her that graduation was just around the corner. Annie had been accepted at Vassar, she'd soon be going off to college. She'd make new friends. The accident would become a forgotten incident in an otherwise memorable school career.

On a hot, steamy day in June of 1984, while the school band played *Pomp and Circumstance*, Annie and I were graduated from Ambrose Academy together with some fifty other seniors, all of us in black caps and gowns. My sister was still wearing the soft cast under her long black gown. None of her graduating team mates came over to congratulate her.

On September sixteenth that year, on a clear bright Sunday morning, we all drove out to Ridley Hills, New Jersey, to witness my brother Aaron's marriage to the "Lack of Manners Clan," as my sister had dubbed Augusta's august tribe.

A week later, Annie flew off to New Delhi.

My mother swore she had not paid for the coach ticket on Air-India.

Neither she nor I could imagine where Annie had got the money for it.

5

That first trip to India and Southeast Asia ended some eight months later. Annie came home in May of 1985 wearing baggy pants and sandals, and silver circlets through her brow, her nostril, and her tongue. Her hair was hennaed and crawling with lice. (Her pubic hair, too, my mother later informed me.) It was after this first journey to India that Annie told us she was a Tantric adept, having been initiated into the religion in Sri Lanka. She brought home a collection of the jewelry she'd learned to make from a silversmith in Bali, an odd collection of earrings, bracelets, pins, and rings fashioned mostly of silver and copper, with one or two pieces in gold. Some of the work depicted Shiva and Shakti, the god and goddess who were Tantric adepts. But most of the jewelry . . .

"Oh dear," my mother said when Annie held up for exhibit a massive gold ring shaped in the form of a penis wrapped around her forefinger, its bulging head set with a tiny seed pearl representing delayed orgasm. We were beginning to understand that "Tantric adept" meant someone skilled in the art of prolonging sexual awareness through ritualized intercourse. We were beginning to catch on to the fact that Annie believed sexual orgasm was a cosmic and divine experience, something my mother didn't particularly relish hearing because she didn't want to believe her young daughter—Annie would be nineteen in September—was running all over the universe prolonging the pleasures of intercourse without reaching orgasm as described in the fourth-century Hindu sex manual called the Kama-sutra.

But spread all over my mother's rug was an assortment of wrought, or perhaps overwrought, penises, vaginas, clitorises, testicles, nipples, and various abstract representations of "orgasms without ejaculation," as Annie described them, silver and gold and copper and bronze splashing drily this way and that in perpetually delayed frenzy. The jewelry was explicitly sexual. In fact, it was embarrassingly so.

"An early Tantric deity was a goddess idolized in the form of the *yoni*," Annie said, "which is the vulva on that pin, Mom."

At that moment, my mother was holding in her hand a copper pin formed in the shape of an open vagina with the shaft and head of a penis lying between its ripened lips.

"The male god was represented by the *lingam,* which was the Aryan word for penis, Mom, you can see that on the pin, too."

"Yes, I see," my mother said, and placed the pin back on the rug as if it had grown suddenly hot in her hand.

"In Tantra," Annie went on to explain, "the sexual partners learn to heighten the act through the use of breath control, proper posture, meditation, and the pressure of fingers. You'll see that one of the rings—which by the way can actually be *used* during sexual intercourse—is shaped like a tiny finger. I used a real ruby for the fingernail."

"Would anyone care for some coffee?" my mother asked.

We were still living on Columbus and Seventy-second at the time. Mr. Alvarez, who was still super of the building, used to keep pigeons on the roof, and Annie and I went up there one evening shortly after her return, to watch the sunset. There were times, when Annie and I were growing up, that we seemed to live in a world of our own, speaking codes we ourselves invented, the ciphers known only to ourselves. But even when we spoke in plain English, it was a rapid form of communication, Annie completing a sentence I had begun, I finishing one of hers. We were a reclusive, self-reliant pair. We needed no one else in our closed and intimate circle. We were twins. That evening, it seemed we were twins again. Annie was home again.

Sitting with our backs to one of Mr. Alvarez's coops, the birds making their soft subtle sounds behind us, she told me that traveling to places like India and Indonesia had been difficult at times, but she knew she'd remember it forever, and felt certain she'd go back again . . .

"I know that with all my heart, Andy."

It was a calm, lovely evening, the end of what had been a surprisingly cool day in June. Dusk was fast approaching in Manhattan, evengloam was almost upon us. When we were children, we used to come up to the roof all the time, to watch the sun set over Manhattan. We used to look to the West, and watch the sun going down behind the GW Bridge. There were hardly any tall buildings on the Jersey shore back then. My sister and I would hold hands as the sun gradually disappeared and dusk gathered. We were holding hands now as well, the pigeons gently murmuring behind us.

"I wish you wouldn't keep running off all the time," I said.

"Oh, don't be silly," she said, "*all* the *time!* I've only been gone twice. And I always come back, don't I? You should come with me next time. You want to be a writer, you'd learn a lot."

"Well, a writer," I said.

"You really would have enjoyed the sex show I went to in Bangkok," she said, and waggled her eyebrows like Groucho Marx. "There was a woman who popped Ping-Pong balls out of her vagina . . ."

"Disgusting," I said.

" . . . and another one who pulled out a series of small metal balls on a chain. Another woman used her vagina to blow a toot on a toy bugle . . ."

"Please, Annie."

"I'm telling you the truth. One woman even stuck a cigarette in there, and lit it, and smoked it. With her vagina! I mean it. Blew smoke rings from her vagina! Anything but what it's meant for, right? God, I hated Bangkok! The air was so polluted, my eyes burned all the time. You know what they do in Thailand, Andy? Pregnant women drink the milk from young coconuts so their babies'll be born with lovely skin, did you know that?"

"You're making all this up."

"No, it's true. They have schools that train monkeys to climb trees to bring down young coconuts."

"What else do they do in Thailand?"

I was smiling. I knew she was inventing all this. I was thinking, She's the one who should become the writer.

She smiled back at me, tapped me playfully on the hand to let me know she was telling the absolute truth. In the West, the sky was already beginning to turn red and orange and yellow.

"The people burn the peels of mandarin oranges to keep mosquitoes away from their houses. So they won't get malaria. That's what I'm going to do the next time I go there. Burn orange peels. Instead of taking those stupid malaria pills."

"I wish you wouldn't go away again," I said.

"You can come with me," she said. "Do you know there's a fine for chewing gum in Singapore?"

"I'll just bet there is."

"Stop it, Andy, I'm *serious!* You can get a fine for chewing *gum!* And in Yo Jakarta, a bell . . . which do you like best, Andy, I've heard it pronounced three ways. Joe Jakarta, Yo Jakarta, and even Georgia Carter, which sounds like a stripper, doesn't it? I prefer Yo Jakarta, it sounds softer, doesn't it, Yo Jakarta? Do you remember the trouble Daddy had with the names in *The Once and Future King?* When he read it to us at bedtime? All those strange medieval names! But in Yo Jakarta, a bell peals at bedtime, to remind the women to take their birth control pills. They sound a second bell an hour later."

"The second one is called *coitus interruptus,*" I said.

Annie laughed.

I knew she was making all this up.

"In Bali," she said, "if a person is buried in the ground, he won't go to heaven. That's why it's important to be cremated. But if you live on the side of a mountain, it's all right for your body to be laid out on the ground to decompose in the sun. That's because mountains are holy."

The sun in the Western sky was rapidly dipping below the horizon. We sat side by side with our backs against the pigeon coops. It was such a good time of day. It was so good to have Annie home again.

"There's a temple in Bali where menstruating women aren't allowed to enter," Annie whispered, as if telling an enormous secret now. "There's a big sign out front, I mean it, this isn't a joke. Because it's a holy place. I'll take you there sometime, it's called Uluwatu, and it's supposed to be full of these little gray monkeys that are holy. I went in, anyway. They told me later I shouldn't have. Because that day, there was only one monkey in the temple, instead of the hundreds that were supposed to be there. In fact, they call it The Monkey Temple. But there was only one monkey that day. Because I had my period, and went in, and angered the gods. Was what they told me later."

"Who told you? The guides?"

"No, not the guides."

"Then who? The gods?"

"Don't be silly."

"Well, who, Annie?"

"I don't remember. Somebody told me. Who remembers? Anyway, what difference does it make? I never listen to what they say."

"What who says?"

"Whoever," she said, and waved one hand on the air, as if brushing away a fly. "I'd go crazy if I listened to them."

I turned to look at her. Her face was stained by the setting sun. In the gathering dusk, she shook her head, and then closed her eyes. Behind us, the pigeons were muttering softly.

"Do you remember when Daddy used to read to us at night?" she asked.

"Oh yes."

"Do you remember when Archimedes the owl taught the Wart to fly?"

"I remember," I said.

The sun was almost gone.

"Do you remember Cully the hawk? And the two falcons, Balan and Balin?"

"Yes, Annie, I remember."

"Do you remember the wild goose Lyo-lyok?"

"Yes, oh yes."

"It used to be such fun," she said. "Flying."

❑

In September of 1985, my sister started a new rock group named The Gutter Rats, and was preparing for a tour through Dixie. A tour!

You have to understand that this so-called rock group was in effect a garage band with pretensions. I don't know how they managed to find a booking agent, and I don't know how he succeeded in getting jobs for them throughout the South, but they did, and he did. His name was Wallace Hennessy, Wally to my sister and the four other members of her group. I met him only once and remember him as a huge and flatulent man in his early forties, wearing a rug that looked like a fright wig.

There was a black girl named Pearl in the group (she played keyboard) and a lead guitarist and bass guitarist who were also black and whose names were either Teddy and Freddie or Perry and Lennie, I forget. There was also a white drummer named Stephen. As she had with The Boppers, the group we formed when we were fifteen, my sister played tambourines and sang. You will remember that in that earlier effort, I played bass guitar, which is the equivalent of choosing geology as the course to fill your science requirement. I mentioned this to either Freddie or Lennie, one old bass-guitar player to another, heh-heh, get it, Fred, Len, little poke in the ribs there, get it? Not a smile.

In January of 1986, Wally booked The Gutter Rats on a tour that ran them through Virginia and the Carolinas, and then swung through Tennessee, Alabama, and Georgia, before heading into Florida where they would play Tampa, St. Pete, and a few towns in the Everglades. As rock bands go, they weren't too bad. They were merely amateurish. In that respect, and again because our lives—my sister's and mine—seem to run all too often along parallel lines, my writing wasn't too bad, either, it was merely amateurish. Or maybe it was bad *and* amateurish. But at least it never got me in trouble. The band did get Annie in trouble.

I was still living at home, and attending school at NYU, when the call from Georgia came that May. My mother answered the phone. It was the middle of the night. Everything with Annie seems to occur in the middle of the night. "Andrew, wake up," my mother yelled, "quick, pick up the phone!"

"What is it?" I said.

"Your sister's in trouble. Annie? Hello, just a minute, your brother's getting the extension. Andrew!" she yelled.

"I've got it," I said.

I was on the living room phone already, standing there in my pajamas. My mother was on the phone in her bedroom.

"Annie? We're both on now. What is it?"

"Hello, Sis."

"Hi."

"What is it, Annie?"

"Nothing," she said. "I got arrested."

"What for?" my mother asked.

"I peed on a policeman."

"You what?"

"He wasn't in uniform."

"Annie, what on earth . . . ?"

"Where are you?" I asked.

"Georgia," she said.

"Where in Georgia?"

"Just outside Atlanta."

"You got arrested?" my mother said.

"It's okay, I'm out on bail."

"But why'd they . . . *what* did you say you did?"

"He forced us to take off our panties."

"Annie!"

"Well, he did, Mom."

"Then *he's* the one they should have arrested."

"Oh sure," Annie said. "I need money to pay the fine, Mom. The gig broke up in a riot, and we never got paid. Can you send me some money?"

"How much money?"

"A thousand dollars."

"What!"

"The fine is a thousand dollars."

"What!"

"This was a cop I pissed on, Mom."

The way she tells it, the party at the fire house was in full swing when this young man came up to the bandstand and made advances. Fire house, you heard me correctly; the jobs Wally Hennessy booked for The Gutter Rats were seldom of high caliber. The job that night (or gig, as my sister preferred calling it) was paying a hundred dollars a man (women, too, for that matter) and started at eight and was to have ended at midnight had it not been for the fracas precipitated by one Harley Welles.

At the time, Pearl Williams was a strikingly attractive black girl who was only a fair musician, as for that matter was every other musician in the group, with the possible exception of my sister whose tambourine-shaking was admittedly no great shakes, but whose voice was pretty good for this level of performance. They made a nice couple, my sister and Pearl. Shaking her tambourines and her considerable booty, Annie would stand emerald-eyed and blond and somewhat body-pierced, belting out songs made famous by other singers, while behind her at the keyboard Pearl tossed her head and hurled lightning bolts from her flying fingers, dark eyes flashing, wide grin promising gospel-sister pleasures. It was no wonder that Harley Welles thought both these ripe young ladies from the big bad city might care to accompany him home for the night.

Harley was wearing some kind of blue nylon jacket with yellow letters on the back, GHP for Georgia Highway Patrol or some such, although the first time around (we heard *this* story many times, too) he was merely an out-of-uniform member of the local constabulary. Whatever else he was, he was certainly comical. At least the way Annie tells it. She's wonderful with accents and dialects, my sister. I wish I could do them the way she does.

Young Harley, it appears, came up to the bandstand during the eleven o'clock break and immediately introduced himself to Pearl and my sister.

"Hah, ah'm Hahley Wales, nice t'meet y'all, ladies."

(I can't do dialects, I'm sorry.)

I've been observing you ladies (he tells them in his inimitable way) and it occurred to me that you both being strangers in town and all, you might enjoy a little sight-seeing tour after y'all quit playing tonight. I want you to know there are more enjoyable places we could visit here in town than this li'l ole fire house, though I must say your presence has enlivened and beautified the place beyond measure. We could, for example, go to a fine ole bar I know of down the road, which is touch-close to a lovely motel many visiting celebrities like y'all stay at when they're here in town. I would be happy—

"We're busy, thanks," my sister says.

"Thanks," Pearl echoes.

I would be happy (young Harley goes on, undeterred) to accompany you ladies to this bar I'm telling you about, where perhaps you might enjoy dancing a little instead of singing and playing your l'il ole hearts out, like you're doing here, though it's a juke box there, I must admit.

I'm a fair dancer, and I would be happy to alternate as your partner, so to speak, until such time as the three of us might become better acquainted. I've been noticing how well you two ladies play together, and I know this sort of intimacy, if you take my meaning, comes with practice—

"Get lost," my sister says.

"But thanks," Pearl says.

He is not about to get lost, young Harley. He tells my sister that if perhaps *she's* not interested, then maybe her little black friend here with the swift fingers and the big smile might be enticed into sharing a brew and tripping the light fantastic, or whatever, this being an enlightened age in the South and all. My sister tells him that perhaps he hasn't understood what she's saying, which is that neither she *nor* her little black friend here with the speedy fingers and the bright smile is interested in sharing anything at *all* with him tonight, and besides it's time they got back on the bandstand.

"So tell you what, Cracker, take a walk," she says. "Or I'll call a cop."

"I *am* a cop," he says.

According to my sister, Harley then pulled a rather large weapon from under his blue nylon jacket with the letters GHP on it, and pointed it at both her and Pearl, waving it in their faces from one to the other, and forcing them to accompany him outside behind the fire house where he ordered both of them to take off their panties and pee on their hands.

This was sixteen years ago.

I had not yet heard Annie's story of molestation by the man giving pony rides or the kid sitting behind her on the saddle or poor Mr. Alvarez under the sink. When she related this Southern atrocity story to me and my mother, it sounded entirely fresh and believable. My mother was thoroughly appalled. I think she would have preferred Annie being raped, rather than so humiliated; her ruination, so to speak, rather than her urination.

As for me, I found the whole tale amusing. First, the image of these two frightened amateur rock artists, one black, one white, pulling down their panties for a redneck in a blue nylon jacket holding a .357 Magnum on them, and then Pearl actually starting to pee on her own talented fingers while Annie becomes so enraged that she suddenly straddles ole Harley's leg and begins pissing all over his pants and his shoes—hey, you can't get that on prime time television.

We laughed so hard, Annie and I.

❏

We sit on the living room sofa, side by side, my mother and I. It is beginning to become light outside, a false dawn promising another clear day. I take my mother's hand in mine. It is cold to the touch.

"Mom," I say, "when did you speak to her last?"

My mother hesitates.

"Mom?"

"Yesterday afternoon sometime. I was going downstairs to do some shopping. We needed milk and orange juice."

"What did she say to you?"

"She certainly didn't say she was planning to leave. I would have . . ."

"Mom? Please, okay? We're trying to find her. No one's hurling accusations. Can you remember what she said?"

My mother sighs deeply.

"She was watching television. I came in to ask if she wanted to come shopping with me. An old movie was playing. Something with Joan Crawford, they play all those old movies in the afternoon. Annie asked me if I thought Joan Crawford was smarter than she was. I told her . . ."

"Smarter? Why would she ask something like that?"

"She said people say Joan Crawford is smarter. People say she's stupid."

"What people?"

"Well, she didn't say 'people,' exactly," my mother says, sounding suddenly wary, even cagey, the way she often sounds when we're discussing my sister.

"What *were* her exact words? Can you remember?"

"Well . . . she asked me if I thought Joan Crawford was smarter than she was, and when I said 'No,' she said, 'They say she's smarter.' "

"They?"

"Yes."

"*They* say?"

"Yes."

"Who did she mean by 'they,' did she say?"

"No. Well . . . she was using it the way everyone uses it. It's a common expression. 'They say' means 'People say.' "

"Did she seem to think anyone was at that very moment telling her Joan Crawford was smarter than she was?"

"No, she was watching television. There were just the two of us in the room. *I* certainly didn't tell her Joan Crawford was smarter."

"What did you tell her?"

"I told her Joan Crawford had script writers."

"She didn't think anyone on *television* was telling her Joan Crawford was smarter, did she?"

"Well, I can't say what she was thinking, I'm not a mind reader."

"Did she seem to be listening to voices coming from the television set?"

"There *were* voices coming from the television set, Andy. There was Joan Crawford's voice and the actress in the scene with her, I forget her name."

"Mother," I say, "please don't be dense."

My mother flashes me one of her withering green-eyed looks.

"I'm asking you if voices told Annie to run off again."

"I did not hear any voices speaking to Annie," she says stiffly. "Did she ever tell you she hears voices?"

"No."

"Then what are you saying?"

"I'm simply trying to . . ."

"There were no voices. Wouldn't I know if she was hearing voices?"

"But she said '*They* say,' is that right?"

"*They* say she's smarter, yes."

"Meaning Joan Crawford."

"Yes."

"And you told her Joan Crawford had script writers."

"Well, first Annie said, 'They think I'm stupid.' "

"*They* again."

"Yes."

"What'd you think she meant by that?"

"People. People think she's stupid. But they don't, you know. All my friends think she's highly intelligent."

"You didn't think she was referring to voices or anything."

"No, I didn't think she was referring to voices or anything, as you put it. Look, son, I know just where you're going, so cut it out, will you, please? Your sister wasn't talking to Joan Crawford or anybody else but me, is what you're suggesting, isn't it? That Annie hears voices? That's right, isn't it? *Annie* hears voices, *I* hear voices, everybody in the whole wide *world* hears voices except you and your Dr. Lang! Please, kiddo, give me a break!"

"Did she say anything else?"

My mother doesn't answer me.

"Mom?"

"I heard you."

"Well, did she?"

"She said, 'Forget it.' "

"And that was it?"

"Yes."

"Was she still watching television when you left the room?"

"Yes."

"Did she say anything when you came back?"

Again, my mother doesn't answer.

"Mom?"

"No," she says at last. "Nothing."

The front door opens.

Augusta is back from her nicotine break.

"Anything happen while I was gone?" she asks, sounding as if she'd been to the ladies' room during a particularly good part of a movie and now wants to know what she missed.

"Andy thinks his sister was talking to Joan Crawford," my mother says.

"I wouldn't be surprised," Augusta says, and then waves her hand as if to dismiss this entire nutty family into which she has married.

"Where's Aaron?" my mother asks. "I thought he was with you."

"He's downstairs chatting with the doorman," Augusta says. "Is there any coffee?"

"On the stove," I say.

"His sister's gone, and he's downstairs chatting with the *doorman?*"

"I'll go get him," I say, and leave the apartment at once.

❑

My brother Aaron is standing outside the building when I come downstairs. He is smoking a cigarette. He looks like all the other lost souls standing outside buildings all over Manhattan, puffing on their forbidden cigarettes. He is the CEO of a giant corporation, but he has been reduced to sneaking smokes behind the barn.

He does not even try to hide the fact from me. Perhaps he's forgotten that he told us he quit smoking five years ago. Or perhaps he no longer gives a damn what he told us. There is certainly an arrogant swagger to the manner in which he deliberately takes a huge puff as I approach, and then blows the smoke on the air like a factory smokestack belching pollutants.

"I thought you quit smoking," I say.

I have never been able to resist taking a jab at Aaron. Perhaps that's because he took so many jabs at me when we were kids. Rarely does his *verbal* sparring match mine, however. This time his riposte is at least adequate.

"So did I," he answers. "What's going on upstairs?"

"Joan Crawford," I say.

"Joan Crawford?"

"Whether or not Annie heard Joan Crawford talking to her."

"I'm sure she did," Aaron says.

I look at him.

"What do you mean?"

"Nothing," he says.

"What makes you so sure Annie . . . ?"

"The doctor in Sicily told you she hears voices, didn't he? So it's quite possible she heard Joan . . ."

"No, you didn't say it was quite *possible,* you said you were *sure.* What makes you so sure all of a sudden?"

"Forget it, okay?"

"No, let's not forget it. Annie's gone . . ."

"Annie's been gone forever," he says, and takes a last drag on his cigarette, and crushes it under his shoe. He is starting into the building when I catch his sleeve.

"Just a second, Aaron."

Our eyes meet.

"What is it you know?"

"Let it go, Andy."

"No. Tell me. Please."

He hesitates a moment, and then shrugs and takes a deep breath.

"How do you think she got the money to go to India that first time?" he asks.

"I always suspected Mama gave it to her."

"Never in a million years. Mama was still angry about the band equipment."

"Then how?"

"Do you remember when it was? That she went to India?"

103

"Yes?"

"A week after my wedding. Do you remember my wedding?"

I remembered it came as no surprise that Augusta decided to get married not in the New York area, where everyone in *our* family lived, but instead in Ridley Hills, New Jersey, where the Unmannerly Clan lived. Never mind that Grandma Rozalia was battling cancer at Sloan-Kettering, never mind that. We were invited to Ridley Hills, and if we couldn't make the long trip there—as certainly Grandma couldn't—then that was unfortunate, kiddies. As Augusta's younger brother The Gulf War Hero once remarked, "In her own way, Augusta leads." Ah yes, so she does.

So on that brisk Sunday morning in September, I rented a car and drove my mother and sister across the George Washington Bridge, and onto the Jersey Turnpike, and then across the entire state of New Jersey to where first Ridley, and next Ridley Falls, and finally Ridley Hills nestled close to the Pennsylvania border. We actually passed the football stadium where Augusta must have conceived on a pair of starlit nights in a Chevy and on the grass. We actually passed the hospital where she gave birth first to Lauren and next to Kelly. We actually found the church—Augusta's directions were somewhat less than meticulous—where she would be bound in holy matrimony to my jackass brother, who was now asking me to remember a day I'd chosen long ago to forget.

"I remember, yes," I said.

"Augusta's father gave us a thousand dollars as a wedding gift."

"Yes?"

"Annie stole it."

"No, she didn't."

"Andy, please, she stole it."

"I don't believe that."

"Believe it, don't believe it. Kelly saw her putting the envelope in her hand bag."

"How old was Kelly? Eight, nine? You took the word of . . ."

"She was ten. And she's my daughter."

"Be that as it may."

"What's that supposed to mean, Andy?"

"It means some ten-year-old *kid* tells you . . ."

"My *daughter,* Andy. Not some ten-year-old *kid.* My *daughter* told me she saw Annie slipping that envelope in her hand bag. And I believed her. Period."

"Fine. What's this got to do with Annie hearing voices?"

"I kept wondering why she'd done such a thing. Annie? Sweet little Annie who used to sit on Daddy's lap when he read to us? How could she steal a thousand bucks from her own brother on his wedding day?"

She *didn't,* I'm thinking. You want an answer? Okay, she didn't. Your daughter was wrong. Or she was lying. Or maybe both. Annie is not a thief!

"Augusta refused to have her in our house after that, can you blame her? But I kept wondering. I mean, this was Annie, my little *sister.* How could she do a thing like that? Then when she got into that mess in Georgia, I started thinking about it all over again. Maybe because she'd stolen a thousand bucks . . ."

"No, she didn't, Aaron."

"Oh yes she did. And the fine in Georgia was a thousand bucks, too, some coincidence, huh? Mama paid the fine, of course. Mama always pays, doesn't she, she never learns."

I'm thinking, *You're* the rich man, Aaron, why don't *you* occasionally bail out our sister? Why do you always leave it to Mama?

"But why just a fine? She *assaults* a police officer, and no charges are brought? No trial? Not even an appearance before a local magistrate? Nothing? Just, hello, goodbye, thanks for visiting Georgia? So I began thinking, Gee, maybe my sister's a thief *and* a liar. Otherwise, why . . . ?"

"She's neither, Aaron."

"Okay, maybe just the voices are liars and thieves."

"How do you know there are voices?"

"Do you remember the Welcome Home party Mama gave her? When she got back from the tour that fall?"

"I remember."

"Pearl Williams was there."

"Pearl . . . ?"

"Who used to play keyboard with the band?" he says. "She told me what *really* happened in Georgia."

❑

In addition to the band itself, and the Gulliver family (minus Augusta, who as usual has matters to take care of in New Jersey) Annie has invited to the party some kids we knew from Ambrose Academy. There are maybe twenty to thirty people in the apartment when she announces that the band will now perform "For your delectation and elucidation," she says, grinning, "a few select tunes from our recently concluded triumphant tour of the South. Pearl?" she says. "Guys?"

The Gutter Rats actually manage to play three full numbers before Mr. Alvarez, the super, comes upstairs to politely ask if we can tone it down a little, he's getting complaints from the neighbors. The band is grateful for the respite. They've been touring all summer, and they've "picked their fingers to the bone," as one of the guitar players tells Aaron. The mood in my mother's apartment on Seventy-second Street is one of celebration and good fellowship, everyone suddenly descending on the dining room table where my mother has set out wine, and sandwiches she herself made for the occasion. My sister flits like a firefly among the members of her band and our former school mates. Aaron takes a chair alongside Pearl.

"It's so good to meet you at last," she says. "Annie's told me such wonderful things about you."

He can't imagine Annie ever having told anyone anything nice about him, but he nods in acknowledgment, raises his wine glass in a silent toast, sips, puts the glass down on the end table beside him, and is picking up his sandwich when Pearl says, "She seems okay now, doesn't she?"

He doesn't know who she means.

"Annie," she explains. "She seems to've gotten over what happened in Georgia."

"Oh, yeah, that was something, wasn't it?" he says.

"Never saw nothin like it in my life," Pearl says, shaking her head. "Her losin it that way."

❑

The way Pearl tells it . . .

But first she takes a sip of her wine, and glances to where Annie is standing chatting with the girl who was co-captain of the soccer team before she broke her leg . . .

The way she tells it, there were no clues that anything might be wrong with Annie until that morning in May, in Atlanta, when she attacked the waitress.

Pearl knows, of course, that Annie has been all over the world. She never ceases telling everyone and anyone about her travels all through Europe and Asia and her spiritualistic explorations and discoveries and eventual conversion to the Tantric religion. Pearl has seen (as who could not?) the silver circlet in Annie's tongue and the other through her left nostril and the third over her right eye, respectively purchased in Katmandu, Hong Kong, and Sri Lanka. Pearl has even seen (they were roommates, after all) the swastika tattooed on Annie's right buttock with the mysterious words *Ek Xib Chac* and *Chac Xib Chac* straddling it in red and in black. Pearl—like my brother Aaron—believes that Annie is a trifle eccentric, but hey, man, most rock musicians are, and for a white chick, she can sing up a fuckin storm. So everything's cool until that morning in May, when suddenly a waitress in a pink uniform in a cheap little diner in a dinky Georgia town outside Atlanta seems threatening to Annie.

Pearl isn't even aware of it at first, she's busy with her sausage and eggs. They were up till two in the morning, and this is now close to noon, and they're sitting opposite each other in one of the booths, neither of them wearing makeup, Annie in a halter top and jeans, Pearl wearing overalls over a white T-shirt. This is 1986, and this is the enlightened South, and a black girl eating yellow scrambled eggs can sit at a table with a white girl licking purple jam off whole wheat toast.

But something is bothering Annie.

Aaron is listening intently now. Presumably, Pearl's tale will lead inexorably to The Urination Incident and the *real* reason my sister got arrested. Across the room, one of the Ambrose girls begins giggling.

"She's watching me," my sister says.

Pearl looks up from her plate.

"Who?" she asks.

"Don't look at her," my sister whispers. "She'll know."

Pearl thinks she's kidding at first. My sister does great imitations, so surely she's doing one of her bits now, pretending to be a fugitive on the run, or an undercover detective, or whatever, her eyes darting toward the counter where a redheaded waitress in a pink uniform is sitting smoking a cigarette and reading a newspaper.

"She knows," my sister whispers.

"Knows what?" Pearl asks. "Who?"

"The waitress. Don't look at her."

Pearl turns to look at her again.

The waitress is not paying them the slightest bit of attention. She looks like any other waitress in any cheap roadside diner anyplace in America.

Annie is suddenly out of the booth.

She goes to the counter.

"I'm onto you," she whispers.

The waitress swivels her stool around. She is facing a young blond girl in blue jeans and a red halter top, nineteen, twenty years old, somewhere in there, rings on her fingers and bells on her toes, standing in front of her with her hands on her hips, green eyes blazing, lips tightly compressed, hissing words through teeth virtually clenched. The waitress doesn't know what she's trying to say or what the hell's bugging her.

Annie slaps the newspaper out of her hands.

"Hey!" the waitress says.

"Stop second-guessing me!" Annie yells.

Pearl is out of the booth, already heading for the counter.

"Hell's wrong with you?" the waitress asks, and is reaching down to pick up her newspaper when Annie shoves out at her, pushing her off the stool. Pearl's eyes go wide. The waitress is screaming bloody murder now, and a white man who looks like he wouldn't at all mind a good old-fashioned lynching comes running from the kitchen with a cleaver in his hands.

"Run!" Annie yells, and is out the front door and onto the street before the short order cook, or whatever he is, can come around the counter with his cleaver. Pearl has been black for twenty-two years. She knows better than to run in Georgia, or Harlem, or Watts, or anyplace else where a running black man is reason enough for somebody white to chop off his legs. She lets the waitress and the short order cook do all the running, but by the time they get out on the sidewalk, Annie is gone.

"That's not the end of the story," Pearl says.

Aaron listens.

Annie is not at the motel they've been living in. The band is supposed to check out at two that afternoon, the van is already packed. They're supposed to be heading on to the next town, where they will rehearse in the fire house, and then perform there later that night. The two guitarists (Freddie and Lennie, it now turns out their names are) want to get going. They're still not sure of several passages in Sade's "Sweetest Taboo," and they feel they are absolutely in dire need of the rehearsal this afternoon. Besides, someone like Annie—who is constantly bragging about her travels all over the world—can certainly find her way from here to the next town they're playing, a scant fifteen or so miles south, as the crow flies. Pearl agrees to move on.

Annie does not show up at the fire house until seven o'clock that night, an hour before they're supposed to start playing. She tells Pearl there's a nationwide manhunt out for her, police cars all over the roads, state troopers stopping automobiles and searching them and even opening trunks, looking for the blonde who assaulted the waitress up on US 1. She tells Pearl she walked through fields of corn and tobacco, keeping off the roads, tells her she barely escaped being raped by four redneck ruffians who'd come upon her while she was peeing in the bushes, tells her she stopped at a sharecropper's shack where the door was opened by a bald giant who'd head-butted her and almost knocked her unconscious. She tells Pearl she finally boarded a bus heading south to Macon, and almost missed getting off at the stop here in town. She tells Pearl she's so happy she got to the gig on time because she knows she has an obligation to the band and the music profession and her own talent.

Harley Welles walks into the fire house during the eleven o'clock break. From the way Pearl describes him, he is a dead ringer for Sven Lindqvist in Stockholm, Sweden, except that he is not a hotel waiter, he is instead wearing the uniform of a Georgia Highway Patrolman. But other than that, he is Sven's doppelganger for sure. Six feet-some inches tall, with green eyes and blond hair, my sister must have thought she'd died and gone to Valhalla. Tossing all caution to the winds—after all, the entire law enforcement community of the United States is out looking for her—she sidles up to this handsome stranger and asks if he'd like to accompany her outside while she has a smoke.

According to Pearl, my sister and the trooper Harley Welles go out back to have a smoke or whatever else. Pearl and the guys are hanging around the bandstand, fending off the multitude of fans fighting for their autographs, oh sure, when suddenly there comes a shriek from the alley behind the fire house. Someone is yelling "Rape!" My sister Annie is yelling "Rape!" Again. More urgently this time. Lennie and Freddie are black, and therefore not eager to go anywhere near the location where a white girl is getting raped, you know whut I'm sayin, bro? Stephen is white, but neither is he too keen about rushing to the scene of a felony in progress. Pearl is black but female and presumably incapable of complicity in a sexual attack. It is she who rushes out the open side door of the fire house into a May night alive with fireflies, and stops dead in her tracks when she sees Annie standing alone against the wall of the fire house, the trooper Harley Welles nowhere in sight.

Annie's skirts are up above her thighs.

She is urinating onto the cement driveway.

She is urinating and talking to herself.

Mumbling the words.

Her eyes wild.

There is no one with her.

She is completely alone and talking to herself.

And then she yells "Rape!" again at the top of her lungs, and pulls up her panties, and drops her skirts, and yells, "No!" again, and when she sees Pearl approaching with her hand outstretched and a plaintive look on her face, she shouts "Get away from me!" but she is not talking to Pearl, she is talking to Christ only knows who. And she yells "Rape!" again and rushes off around the back of the fire house and into the arms of two local policemen in uniform and one state trooper named Harley Welles, who apparently ran for backup the minute Annie started behaving peculiarly.

"They wanted to take her straight to jail," Pearl tells him now, "but I begged them not to. I told them she'd just broken up with her boyfriend and was taking it very hard. They didn't believe me for a minute. I think they figured she'd dropped acid or something. But they were nice guys, actually, and they let her off with just a warning instead of booking her for disorderly conduct and inciting to riot, which was what one of the cops said they could've done."

"Well, they weren't *that* nice," Aaron says. "They fined her a thousand bucks."

"Where'd you get that idea?" Pearl asks.

"My mother sent her a thousand dollars."

"Not to pay any fine. How could there be a fine? They never even arrested her."

Aaron looks at her.

"She was lucky, actually," Pearl says.

"Yes."

"It was scary, I have to tell you."

"I'm sure it was."

They sit in silence for several moments. Across the room, there is more laughter.

"But she's okay now, right?" Pearl says.

"Oh, yes, she's fine," Aaron says.

"Well, good," Pearl says. "Good."

Annie walks over, smiling.

"You guys getting to know each other?" she asks.

❑

"You learned this sixteen years ago?" I say.

"Uh-huh."

"You've known this for the past sixteen *years?*"

"Yes, Andy. However long. When she came back from the tour."

"Does Augusta know?"

"I tell Augusta everything."

"No wonder she treats Annie the way she does."

"That's not why she treats Annie however you may think she treats her. But see? You *still* don't believe she stole that money!"

"Who else did you . . . ? Jesus, you didn't tell *Mama,* did you?"

"Yes, I did," Aaron says.

"Then . . . why didn't you tell me?"

"I think you know why, Andy. Besides, what difference would it have made?"

"We might have prevented what happened in Sicily."

"Oh, really? How? Would you have called the police? Would you have put your twin sister away? Who are you kidding?"

"You should have told me."

"I don't think so."

"You should have at least given me a chance," I say, and turn abruptly and start walking away from him.

"Hey!" he calls. "Where're you going?"

"There's someone I have to see," I say, and keep walking.

6

Augusta has two older sisters, a younger brother, and a still-living father and mother. Her father suffered a stroke three years ago, and is in a nursing home. Her mother is a sprightly old lady who knows how to bake strudel. One of the older sisters is divorced and has three children, all of them legitimate, two of them married with children of their own. The other sister is still married, but childless. She's supposed to be a play producer, but I don't know of anything she's ever produced.

Her husband is a theatrical agent and a supposed expert on wines. For Christmas the year before Maggie and I divorced, we sent Aaron and Augusta a bottle of Montrachet Grand Cru imported by Joseph Drouhin for the Marquis de Laguiche estate. The owner of our liquor store told us it was "a wine best drunk young," certainly within five years. It cost us three hundred and twenty-five dollars, which is *some* bottle of white wine, believe me. Augusta's brother-in-law, the wine maven, advised her to "put the wine down" and not drink it for fifteen to twenty years.

Augusta's only brother is single and in the Air Force. He became a hero during the Gulf War, and was immediately thereafter deified by Augusta, who will boast about him at great length if you ever give her the chance. I never give her the chance. Otherwise, she will also bend my ear about her older sister's married children, and *their* children and anyone even remotely related to the Manners family.

As a bizarre example of family solidarity, two or three years ago Augusta discovered that her darling daughter Kelly's roommate—her *roommate*, mind you—was a distant cousin of someone who taught with me downtown, and this automatically bestowed honorary Manners Family status on both Kelly's roomy *and* this math teacher colleague of mine, a nerd if ever there was one, who forever after kept asking me if I'd like to have a beer with him after school.

On the day after the World Trade Center attack, I called Aaron at his office to see how he was. Let it be known that Aaron's office is on Fifty-seventh and Madison, and the school at which I teach is just off Canal Street, not too distant from where everything was happening that day. Aaron immediately began telling me that Augusta's sister's daughter Julianna, their niece whom I'd never in my entire life met, worked in the North Tower, and was twenty minutes late to work that morning because she had a dental appointment, thereby narrowly missing the first plane attack. Not a word about How are you, were you anywhere close at the time, is Mom okay, does Sis know what happened, nothing like that. Just all this shaking of the head and wringing of the hands over *Julianna's* narrow escape, and then a long mournful monologue on the vagaries of fate. I thanked him for his concern, and he actually said, "Hey, what are brothers for, anyway?"

I walk away from him now with my fists clenched, thinking of Augusta and her goddamn family, thinking of the bottle of wine that had cost me half a week's salary, thinking of the nerd math teacher who kept asking me to have a beer with him, thinking of Julianna whom I'd never met and never hoped to meet, thinking of Aaron keeping his secret for sixteen years, hiding from me the fact that my twin sister pissed in public and held a running dialogue with a non-existent person or persons who were attacking her!

I am furious with him.

And with myself as well.

How could I have missed it?

How could I not have known?

Or have I really known all along?

❏

My sister Annie has told me at least a hundred times that she can recall her entire life as if it is on a loop of film. She can play the loop backward or forward, stopping it on any frame she wishes, calling up memories at will.

My own memory is not as accommodating.

But I can remember . . .

I can remember . . .

Maggie and I meeting on a bus.

This was in the fall of 1988. I was almost twenty-two years old and a senior at New York University. In fact, I was heading downtown to school. As soon as I graduated in June, I planned to leave for Paris, where I would become Ernest Hemingway. When I sat down beside her, I forgot all about Paris.

She was wearing blue jeans and a rust-colored turtleneck sweater that day. Black hair falling to her shoulders. Eyes lowered, reading *The Man Who Mistook His Wife for a Hat*. Long black lashes. An exquisitely turned nose in a fine fox face, all high cheeckbones and swift jaw line and patrician brow. Altogether the most beautiful woman I'd ever seen in my entire shaggy bespectacled English-major life.

I dared.

"Any good?" I asked.

She turned to look at me. Raised her eyes to me. Eyes as black as chimney soot.

"Very," she said, and went back to her book.

I had never heard of the book. I thought it was a comic novel. I tried to think of something brilliant I could say to this utterly exquisite creature engrossed in a comic novel as the bus sped her to whatever her destination might be, where she would step down onto the sidewalk and out of my life forever, but I was completely tongue-tied in her presence. I could not understand this. I was normally a somewhat garrulous student of English Literature at NYU.

"Listen," I said at last, "I want to marry you."

She turned to me again. Patiently. She raised her eyes. A slight smile formed on her mouth. Such a beautiful, lovely, stunning, gorgeous mouth with sticky red lipstick all over it.

"Oh do you?" she said.

Faintly amused. I hoped.

Or would she hit me on the head with her book?

"First tell me your name," I said.

"Maggie," she said.

"Maggie, I love you."

"Have *you* read this book?" she asked.

"No, is it funny?"

"You should read it. I think you may be mistaking me for your hat."

"*Will* you marry me?" I said.

"Not just now, but thanks anyway."

(In the story later based on our meeting, a black guy sitting behind us says, "For Pete's sake, marry him, lady." This did not happen. And the story never sold. It was called "Bus Ride." I think maybe the title was too close to "Bus Stop.")

"Maggie," I said, "would you like to have a cup of coffee instead?"

(In real life, there actually was a black man sitting not behind us but across the aisle. He did not pay us the slightest bit of attention.)

This time, she looked me over.

I am not a particularly attractive man. I do not know what Maggie saw in me that day on that bus hurtling downtown too fast through crowded city streets to a destination that would take her out of my life for all time. I never could imagine what she continued to see in me during the three years of our marriage. My sister is the beautiful twin. I am merely a washed-out impression of her, my blond hair what used to be called "dirty," my nose a trifle too long for my face, my green eyes (my sister's sparkle like emeralds) too pale and less than compelling behind glasses I've worn since I was ten. I don't know what she saw in me, but she saw something.

She would later rue the day.

But on that September fifth, in the year of our Lord nineteen hundred and eighty-eight, Maggie nodded slowly and said, "Yes, I would like to have a cup of coffee instead."

❏

It starts over coffee, it ends over coffee.

We went to a little shop on First Avenue, close to Volumes and Tomes. This was the first surprise. Maggie From the Bus was Maggie Knowles, who in turn was Margaret Katherine Knowles who—at the age of twenty-four, two years older than I—was the proud owner and proprietor of a bookshop called Volumes and Tomes.

"So why would a rich lady like you . . . ?"

"Rich lady, ho-ho."

" . . . want to marry someone like me?" I asked.

She looked across the table at me. I thought she'd say something smart like "Hey, Buster, back off, we're just having a cup of coffee here."

Instead, she said, "I don't know why."

Which meant she *was* going to marry me, of course.

I reached across the table and took her hands in mine. She did not pull them away. I smiled and nodded. She smiled and nodded back.

Actually—though we did not realize this at the moment—there were very good reasons for us to marry each other. To begin with, we looked good together. The classic beauty and the messy would-be writer. Maggie was the one you saw framed at the Met in all those medieval portraits, the long black hair and dark mysterious eyes, the porcelain complexion, the creamy white bosom swelling above a fur-trimmed velvet bodice, I should have tried writing historical romances before I quit writing altogether. And I beside her (though not hanging in the Met), Andrew Gulliver, my muddy blond hair unkempt, my glasses tilted at a rakish Harry Potter angle (though he had not yet been dreamt of back in 1988), my corduroy trousers rumpled, my favorite red maroon sweater somewhat frazzled.

We looked good together.

I fancied myself not the absent-minded nerd, which I sometimes was, but instead the emerging poet, this despite the fact that in my entire life I'd written only one poem, and that a sonnet to Maggie.

> No trace of gold does Maggie's hair reveal
>   Nor can I say it's auburn and be just
> No, it's a raven helmet rolled of steel
>   That shimmers black without a trace of dust.
>
> How often had I dreamt her stunning face
>   Those dazzling eyes, that gorgeous nose and mouth
> To find it there at last upon a bus
>   That raced us through the city north to south.

(By the way, I knew even then that "face" and "bus" did not rhyme. But I considered their mating a sort of slant rhyme, if you will. Besides, I felt I had more than compensated for this truly slight lapse with the internal "raced" rhyme that followed in the last line of the stanza.)

> How long will Maggie's beauty still enchant?
>   How long will our love like a beacon shine?
> To speak for her, I pray you, no, I can't.
>   But let me speak my heart, for it is mine.

Forever, yes, forever and yet more.
Till death us part upon some distant shore.

(I also liked the sort of internal "yes" and "yet" rhyme in the closing couplet. All in all, I felt I'd written a fair example of a sonnet, twelve lines, iambic pentameter, ABAB, CDCD, EFEF, with a rhyming GG couplet at the end. Perfect. Except it was lousy. To everyone but Maggie. She thought it was magnificent. So let me not to the marriage of true minds admit impediments.)

It was Maggie who kept insisting that I write. This was another good reason to get married. Her own self-imposed hours at the shop were horrendous, which gave me a lot of time to myself. I spent that time writing. In the year before our marriage, I must have written two dozen short stories and three chapters to a novel I never finished. During that time, my sister was in India again.

She wasn't even home for our wedding.

❑

The family was beginning to recognize that Annie was a world traveler. Moreover, there seemed to be a pattern to her comings and goings. She would fly off hither and yon, stay in one place for a month or two, move on to another place where she would live for a while on the money my mother kept sending her, and then move on again in search of yet another guru or yet another location for the jewelry shops she opened and closed with alarming frequency. At last, she would come back to New York to settle in with my mother again, something Mama began to appreciate less and less as the years went by. Her longest trip—her second one to India—ended in the spring of 1990.

One sunny Saturday morning, Annie took a taxi from my mother's apartment, where she'd been staying for the past several weeks, and showed up at our apartment with a suitcase. She hugged us both, told us how we should be seeing more of each other now that she was home, and then asked if it would be all right if she spent a few days with us before "heading up to Maine to see what it's like up there."

The next day, we learned why she was really there.

"You can do a promotion linking my work to the Kama-sutra," she told Maggie. "Build like a pyramid of books with my jewelry displayed in front of it."

"Gee, Annie, I don't think that would work for my shop," Maggie said. "I don't even carry the Kama-sutra."

"I'm sure you can order copies. You'd probably sell a ton of them. And you'd be helping me a lot, too."

"It's just that my space is limited . . ."

"Oh, come on, we can always find space."

"And my clientele isn't into . . . uh . . . you know, Oriental religions."

"How about jewelry? Are they into jewelry? We can forget the Kama-sutra, if that's what's bothering you. Just let me set up a little table someplace in the shop."

"It's just that I've never sold jewelry before, Annie. Volumes and Tomes is a book shop, you see. It would seem odd if I suddenly started selling jewelry."

"Well, gee, I don't really think my jewelry is *odd*."

"No, no, neither do I. My *selling* it would be odd. In a book shop. People don't normally look for jewelry in a book shop."

"What's so *ab*normal about putting up a small table with jewelry on it? Look, if it's the *content* of the work . . ."

"The content is a bit explicit, but . . ."

"Well, you don't have to be condescending, really. If it's the erotic content that's bothering you . . ."

"No, that has nothing to do with . . ."

" . . . you can shake hands with the rest of the world, believe me. I've had people walk into my shop, and look around, and then turn up their noses when they recognize a penis or a vagina. If that's the case here, just say so, I won't be offended, really."

"It's just I'm a small independent bookseller . . ."

"Oh, sure, forget it. But Tantra isn't all about sex, you know, it's not some kind of free-love cult. Tantra is a Sanskrit word, in fact. It means to expand or extend, to manifest, to release a cosmic *weave* into the universe. By inspiring our innate sensual spirituality, Tantra awakens and liberates upwardly-motivated energies, allowing us to realize worldly ambitions. So this wouldn't be some kind of uninhibited sex show, Maggie, on the contrary. But look, forget it. We probably wouldn't have time to do it, anyway. I'll be leaving for Maine in a few days."

The few days stretched into a week and then ten days, and Annie was still with us. Maggie and I were living at the time in a small apartment above Volumes and Tomes. You entered into a tiny foyer and then there was a pocket kitchen on the left and a small dining room dead ahead, and then a living room and two bedrooms beyond. Our bedroom faced the building's back yard. The adjoining second bedroom—which also doubled as a storeroom for books—was where we put up Annie. The three of us shared a bathroom nestled between the two bedrooms.

At night, as Maggie and I lay side by side in bed, we could hear my sister next door, reciting her mantras, repeating over and over again what sounded to us like nonsense syllables, but which she said served to concentrate and redirect spiritual energy by eliminating or silencing the mind.

"*Om Mani Padme Aum,*" we heard over and again, coming through the paper thin walls, "*Om Mani Padme Aum, Om Mani . . .*"

Which Annie literally translated for us as "The jewel is in the lotus." Or, in other words, "The *lingam* is in the *yoni.*" Or, more simply put, "The penis is in the vulva." But, hey, Tantra wasn't all about sex, right?

"I know you love your sister," Maggie whispered in my ear, "but I'm not sure I can stand another *minute* of this."

"She'll be gone in a few days," I whispered.

But she wasn't.

❑

Under the best of circumstances, Annie would not have been an ideal house guest. She left dirty bras and panties on the bathroom floor, presumably hoping Maggie would toss them into the wash whenever she laundered her own. She never washed her own dirty dishes either, eating whatever meal she'd cooked for herself, and then leaving dishes and utensils on the dining room table, dirty pots and pans in the sink. Nor did she ever volunteer to do the marketing or take out the garbage, or clean the apartment, even though both Maggie and I were out working all day long.

In the evening, Annie smoked marijuana as part of her daily chakra-puja or "circle worship," the basic Tantric religious ceremony, lacking—in Annie's case—only other worshippers and a guru. The grass was a mind-enhancing soma that was supposed to precede four other Tantric "enjoyments," as she called them. Three of these involved the consumption of various exotic grains, meats, and fruits Annie bought in Chinatown. The fourth was supposed to be sexual intercourse with a male worshipper . . .

" . . . but unfortunately I haven't got one handy just now," Annie said. "Maybe I'll find one up in Maine."

After she smoked her pot, and enjoyed her other three Tantric delights, she put on her nightgown—a long cotton one she'd bought in India—went into her bedroom to say her mantras and was promptly asleep by nine o'clock. This meant she got up early every morning, and was once again reciting her *Oms* and *Aums* before either Maggie or I was awake. I didn't mind this too much. My teaching day started at eight A.M., anyway. But Maggie didn't open the shop till ten, and she didn't appreciate being awakened at the crack of dawn by my sister's incessant chanting.

All in all, it was a difficult time for both of us, and we were delighted when Annie said she'd be leaving for Maine that coming Saturday. As it happened, an author named Carlo Zannetti was coming to do a reading and signing in the shop on Friday night, so Maggie proposed a farewell dinner in the apartment afterward. Annie was thrilled when she learned that Mr. Zannetti was a hypnotist, and that he'd written a book called *MindSet*.

"I can't wait to meet him," she said.

❑

In the eight months and a bit more of our marriage, Maggie and I had developed a sort of *laissez-faire* attitude when it came to routine household chores. Since we both worked, any task that needed doing was usually tackled by whoever could find the time to do it. We never even discussed such matters. See an unmade bed? Make it. Spot a pile of dishes in the sink? Wash them. It was as simple as that. We were truly partners.

So while I was off teaching that Friday, Maggie did all the marketing for our dinner. And when I got home late that afternoon, we both worked side by side in the kitchen, slicing and dicing the ingredients for our salad, mixing an oil and vinegar dressing, scrubbing the potatoes I would later bake (for some peculiar reason, I have always had an aversion to mashed potatoes, gee, I wonder why). Maggie had one eye on the clock. She was supposed to meet Mr. Zannetti in the shop downstairs at five-thirty. We were salting and spicing the lamb chops I would later pop into the oven, when my sister breathlessly rushed into the apartment and locked the door behind her.

"They're here," she whispered.

Maggie must have thought she was referring to the people who'd be attending the book shop event. But that wasn't due to start till six, and it was still only five-fifteen.

"That's okay," she said. "I still have fifteen minutes."

"The ones from Charing Cross," Annie said.

"Who do you mean, honey?"

"When I had the shop there."

"What about it?" I asked.

On her way over to India this time, she had stopped over in London,

125

and had briefly opened a shop exhibiting her own jewelry. The shop closed in three months, after which Annie moved on again. But while it was still functioning, she now told us, a pair of men in blue jackets with the letters FBI in yellow on the back came to visit her one day, pretending to be interested in her jewelry, but really there to check up on Sally Jean.

"Who's Sally Jean?" I asked.

"She was my roommate when I was living in Amsterdam," Annie said. "She used to do translations for the UN. That's why they're so interested in her."

"Who, Annie? Who's interested in her?"

"The FBI! Are you *listening* to me, or what? They're downstairs! They followed me here."

"You're saying there are FBI agents . . ."

"The same ones from Charing Cross," Annie insisted. "After the FBI left that time, some skinheads in tight pink trousers showed up, you could see the outline of their genitals and all, it was awful."

"Sounds good to me," Maggie said, and winked.

"This wasn't funny, Magg. They stood outside on the sidewalk, outside the front window, making threatening gestures, you know, running their fingers across their throats, you know, like slitting their throats? To indicate they were going to kill me?"

"She's serious," Maggie said to me.

"Oh, you bet I am. These people don't play games. They're after Sally Jean, and they want to know what I know about her. It's the same as what happened on the Air France flight from Paris to Luxembourg, when a female agent . . ."

"Annie, slow down," I said.

"I'm sure I told you about the female FBI agent who reached over from the seat behind me and kept my arms pinned . . ."

"No, you never . . ."

" . . . while two big male agents carrying nine-millimeter Glocks boarded the plane and demanded to see my credentials. They carried me off the plane in handcuffs, Andy, I'm *sure* I told you all this."

"No, I don't remember your . . ."

"They took me to a secret room and examined all my orifices. They told me they were looking for contraband narcotics, but who knows what they were *really* doing? They have ways of eavesdropping, you know. They have these little transmitters. Whatever they did to me that time in Luxembourg, it worked. They were able to trace me here, weren't they?"

"Annie," Maggie said, "there is no way a pair of FBI agents . . ."

"*Three* of them this time! Right downstairs!"

" . . . would go marching around New York advertising themselves in jackets that say FBI on the back."

"The two from Charing Cross and another one I never saw before!"

"Okay, I'll go downstairs and talk to them, okay?" Maggie said. "I'll tell them to get the hell away from my shop."

"No! Stay here! I don't want you getting mixed up in this!"

"If somebody's stalking you," I said, "let's call the police."

"No, they're probably in on it, too."

"The police? Why would they . . . ?"

"The UN is here in New York, isn't it? And Sally Jean used to do translations for them."

"Well, then I'll explain that you're entirely innocent in this matter. *You* never did translations for the UN, did you?"

"No, but I know things about the health care system."

"I doubt the FBI . . ."

"Oh, that's what you think."

" . . . *or* the NYPD would be interested in your experience as a candy striper at Lenox Hill."

"You'd be surprised."

"Then what would you like me to do, Annie? Tell me what you'd like me to do, and I'll do it."

"I know you will."

"So tell me, okay? What do you want me to do? Go down and break their eyeglasses?"

"They're not wearing eyeglasses."

"Break their arms? That'll cost you more."

"How much?" she asked at once.

"Arms and legs are a dollar apiece. *Or . . .*" I narrowed my eyes and lowered my voice to a whisper. "I can always terminate them with extreme prejudice."

"Yes, do it," she said.

"Later. Meanwhile, let's put some oregano on these chops, okay?"

"This isn't funny, I don't know why you think it's funny," she said, and turned away swiftly and ran down the hall and into her bedroom. We heard her locking the door behind her. The clock on the wall read five-twenty-five.

"I have to go down," Maggie said. "Will she be all right?"

"Yeah, sure, go ahead."

"Well . . . okay," she said, and glanced at me, and then left the apartment.

❑

Annie did not come out of the bedroom until the signing was over and Maggie brought our guest upstairs. The usual routine was for an author to read for fifteen to twenty minutes, take questions from the audience for the next half-hour or so, and then sign books for another half-hour. The events usually broke up sometime between seven-thirty and eight. Maggie planned to bring Mr. Zannetti upstairs as soon as the shop cleared. We'd have a drink and then sit down to the sumptuous (I hoped) meal I'd prepared.

Well, the event was a spectacular success. The Q and A went on for forty minutes, and almost everyone in the shop—some fifty people in all—bought books. Moreover, Zannetti was a generous man who chatted up anyone who wanted a book signed, so he and Maggie did not come up to the apartment until almost nine o'clock, by which time I had consumed two glasses of red wine.

Carlo Zannetti turned out to be a rotund little man with a small mustache that curled upward at either end, giving the impression that he was perpetually smiling. He was not, as I'd mistakenly surmised, Italian. That is to say, his grandfather had been born in Italy, yes, but both his parents and he himself had been born in Philadelphia, where he still lived. The "Carlo" was a tribute to the grandfather he'd never met; Zannetti was called "Charlie" by everyone he knew.

Charlie's eyes were the only indication that he might be a hypnotist. Large and brown, overhung by black eyebrows shaggier than his small smiling mustache, they seemed capable of peering into a person's very soul. Annie took to him at once.

"Did you hypnotize anyone tonight?" she asked.

"No, no," Charlie said. "I never do that in an uncontrolled venue."

"What do you mean, uncontrolled?"

"Well, I don't think anyone *expected* to be hynotized tonight. That wasn't why they were there."

"We didn't advertise Charlie as a hypnotist," Maggie said. "His book isn't about hypnotism."

"It isn't?" Annie said, surprised.

"It's about making the most of one's potential," Maggie said.

"Sounds like Tantra," Annie said.

"More salad, anyone?"

"Thank you," Charlie said. "Actually, it's about realizing the power of the mind."

"That's what I meant," Maggie said. "Potential. Power."

"Well, that's hypnotism, isn't it?" Annie said. "Controlling someone else's mind?"

"No, no," Charlie said. "In any case, I meant realizing the power of one's *own* mind."

"But you said you wanted a controlled venue."

"Yes, it works best if people come with the expectation of being hypnotized. I don't like surprises, I don't like secrets."

"Secrets?" Annie asked.

"I'll do a corporate speech, for example, and we'll all be sitting down to lunch afterward, and the CEO will suddenly stand up, and clink his glass for attention, and announce, 'I've got a surprise for you! Mr. Zannetti also *hypnotizes* people!' And I'm supposed to get up and turn an account executive into a chicken."

"But that's what you do, isn't it?" Annie said.

"I have on occasion caused people to cackle, yes," Charlie said, and smiled and lifted his wine glass. "Maggie," he said, "here's to you and your beautiful shop and the lovely event you planned for me. I appreciate it sincerely."

"And here's to you for providing an unforgettable evening," Maggie said graciously.

"How about the chef who prepared this unforgettable dinner?" I said.

"Let's hear it for the chef," Maggie said.

"Can you make *me* cackle like a chicken?" Annie asked.

"Now why would a beautiful girl like you wish to cackle like a chicken?" Charlie asked.

"Girl, gee, thank you," Annie said, and smiled. "But seriously. *Can* you hypnotize me?"

"Annie, please," Maggie said. "Charlie's been on for the past two hours, give him a break."

"Or isn't this a controlled venue?" Annie asked.

"This is definitely not a controlled venue," Charlie said. "A controlled venue is a space filled with people who've come there expressly to be hypnotized. Or to see someone else hypnotized. The larger the space, the more people there are, the greater chances of success. If I have a hundred people in an audience, I may find ten who are good subjects. That's a ten percent chance of success. If I have a *thousand* people in an audience, I'll get a hundred and fifty good subjects. The odds go up exponentially."

"Am I a good subject?" Annie asks.

"I have no idea."

"Well, how can you tell?"

"She wants to be hypnotized, Charlie."

"I just want to know how it *works,* Andy. Controlling another person's mind."

"It isn't about control at all," Charlie said. "A hypnotist enters into a partnership with his subject. In a sense, all hypnosis is really *self-*hypnosis. All I am is a coach of the imagination."

"That's lovely," Maggie said. "You should have been a writer."

We all laughed. Except Annie.

She leaned closer to Charlie.

"But if you turn someone into a chicken, you're actually controlling her mind, aren't you?"

"There is no way I can turn the CEO of a giant corporation into a chicken," Charlie said. "He simply will not allow himself to become that. If someone allows herself to cluck like a hen, then deep inside her unconscious there's a sense of playfulness, perhaps a need for role playing. All I do is help that person tap the unconscious. In much the same way that we all conduct inner dialogues with ourselves . . ."

"Inner dialogues?" Annie asked at once.

"Self-talk," Charlie said. "The things we say to ourselves inside our head."

"I don't say anything to myself inside my head," Annie said, and laughed.

"Oh well, of course you do," Charlie said. "We all do."

"Not me."

"What's this sudden interest in hypnosis, anyway?" I asked.

"I've always been interested in it."

"We're subjected to hypnosis every day of the week," Charlie said. "We just don't realize it."

"What do you mean?" Annie asked.

"Politicians, religious leaders, faith healers, television commentators, even novelists . . ."

"Better not invite any more novelists to the shop, Maggie."

"They all try to sway people through the power of suggest . . ."

"Television commentators?" Annie asked. "Can you hypnotize a person through a television set?"

"I meant that figuratively."

"What I'm asking is can you exert power over a person's mind by beaming something at her from a television set?"

"No, I don't think so. Not in the sense that . . ."

"Well, you yourself used the word 'power.' "

"The power of suggestion, yes. Concentrate on that other word. 'Suggestion.' "

"Are you hypnotizing me now?" Annie asked, somewhat flirtatiously, I thought.

"You would know if I were," Charlie said.

"Because you told me to concentrate, you know . . ."

"Yes, look deep into my eyes," Charlie said playfully, and passed his hand over her face like Mandrake the magician.

"Bad man," Annie said. "Next you'll tell me to go kill somebody."

"Hypnotists can't do that, can they?" Maggie said. "Force people to do something against their will?"

Annie was nodding. "Control people's minds," she said. "Transmit thoughts to them."

"We cannot force anyone to do anything he would not do . . ."

"Is that 'he' generic?" I asked.

"He or *she*," Charlie corrected. "We cannot force *them* to . . ."

"Compounding the felony," I said, and winked at Maggie, who didn't get it because grammar was not her strong point.

"We cannot force *anyone*," Charlie persisted, "to do something he or she would not normally do."

"Normally," Annie repeated.

"Normally, yes. But we *can* manipulate reality."

"Meaning?"

"I can hand you a forty-five-caliber pistol, for example, and regress you to the age of five, and tell you the weapon is in reality a water gun, and suggest that you playfully squirt it at your brother here . . ."

"I wouldn't do it," Annie said. "I'd know it was a real gun."

"Perhaps. There are many hypnotists who believe a person never goes under completely. A part of the mind retains control . . ."

"Control again, see?" Annie said. "I find that very scary."

"Well, it is scary," I said.

"I mean, suppose somebody out there has *already* hypnotized all of us . . ."

"Annie, that's science-fiction!" Maggie said, and glanced at me pleadingly, her eyes urging a change of topic.

"No, it isn't!" Annie insisted. "He just told us he can make us believe a forty-five is a *water* pistol!"

"Can he make us believe an Entenmann's pie is a baked Alaska?" I asked.

"All I'm saying is, if it's true someone can transmit messages . . ."

"No, I didn't say . . ."

" . . . that tell me to do something I don't *want* to do . . ."

"No one can do that, dear lady."

"Then how can I protect myself?" Annie asked.

"Just say no," Maggie said.

We all laughed again.

Except Annie.

❑

Maggie waited until she was sure my sister had finished her mantras and was asleep. Then she rolled over next to me and put her mouth close to my ear, and whispered, "Andy? Are you awake?"

"Yes," I whispered back. "What is it?"

"Andy . . . I think there's something wrong with your sister."

"No, no. She just wanted to know about hypnotism, that's all."

"I don't mean just tonight. Though that was strange, too, don't you think? Her being afraid of someone controlling her mind?"

"Well, it is sort of frightening, I think so, too. That you can convince someone a pistol . . ."

"I meant . . . Andy . . . please . . . I know she's your sister . . . but . . . don't you think all that FBI stuff was strange? She seemed to be saying that someone had . . . I don't know . . . surgically implanted a transmitter or something. She picked up on it tonight, too . . ."

"I never heard her say anyone had implanted . . ."

"All that stuff about them taking her to a secret room and examining all her orifices, didn't you hear her use that word? She was trying to tell us they'd . . . I don't know. Don't you remember her saying the FBI has little transmitters? That this is how they eavesdropped on her? Andy, I'm sure she thinks they did something to her in Luxembourg . . ."

"No, she doesn't."

"Yes, she does. She thinks that's how they traced her here."

"You're misreading what she said."

"Andy, she seemed terrified!"

"Well, if somebody was stalking *me,* I'd be . . ."

"She said it was the FBI. She specifically said the FBI!"

"Shhhh, you'll wake her up."

"And tonight she wanted to know if someone could beam commands to her from a tele . . ."

"No, she didn't say that, Maggie."

"She was worried about thoughts being transmitted to her from a *television* set, yes! Where *were* you, Andy? Didn't you hear any of this?"

"Shhhh!"

The bedroom went silent.

Maggie was still for a very long time.

Then she said, "I think she should see someone."

"What do you mean?"

"I think she needs help."

"No, come on."

"You're her brother," Maggie said. "Take her to get help, Andy."

"Well."

"Andy?"

"Yes, Magg?"

"Do you hear me?"

"Let me think about it," I said.

She was silent for several seconds.

Then she said, "Good night, Andy."

"Good night, honey."

Next door, I could hear Annie's gentle breathing.

7

Two days before Christmas Annie called from Maine to say she was going to be all alone on Christmas Day, and if she didn't have such a bad cold she would help serve meals to the homeless but she didn't want to be spreading her germs, so what should she do?

My mother was off skiing, and Aaron and his family were spending the holidays with Augusta's mother in New Jersey (great surprise!) so what *could* we do but invite Annie to come down and stay with us? Actually, I was the one who did the inviting.

"I'm not sure I want her here again," Maggie said.

"It's just for a few days," I said. "It's Christmastime, Magg. Where's your Christmas spirit?"

"Honey, please. I don't want her here. I don't want FBI agents chasing her up Second Avenue again."

"Come on, FBI agents."

"Well, it's what she told us, isn't it?"

"Well, she *did* live with a translator for the UN, you know, so it's entirely possible . . ."

"Oh, now *you* think the FBI is after her?"

"Of course not. Nobody's *after* her, per se. I'm just suggesting that security checks are routine when . . ."

"How about the radio transmitter in her cooze? Is that routine, too?"

"She never said she had a radio trans . . . and really, Magg, I find that vulgar."

"Well, gee, I'm sorry, but it's not *my* cooze that has a radio transmitter buried in it."

"Look, what's the big deal here? She wants to come down for Christmas. I really can't understand what the big . . ."

"Do what you want to do, okay? She's your sister, invite her, don't invite her. But I promise you, if she starts talking about FBI agents again, I'm calling Bellevue."

"She won't start talking about FBI agents."

"Good. Cause I'll have you *both* put away," Maggie said.

"Sure, sure."

"Sure, sure," she said.

❑

Annie came down by train on Christmas Eve.

She was bundled in a blue ski parka and long muffler with alternating blue and red stripes wrapped several times around her neck, and a blue woolen watch cap pulled down around her ears. Her cheeks were red and her eyes were watery, but I thought that was due less to her professed cold than to the frigid weather we were experiencing. I took her duffel and tossed it into the trunk of the taxi, and we drove back to the apartment where Maggie had made a roaring fire (albeit of cannel coal) in the dining room fireplace. We drank homemade soup and ate thick buttered bread, and went to bed shortly before midnight. Annie didn't do her mantras that night. The next morning, she was running a temperature of a hundred and four degrees, and shaking from head to toe.

We were still living in the apartment over the store. The closest hospital was Beth Israel, on First and Sixteenth. In the taxi on the way there, Maggie asked my sister if her medical insurance was up to date. I mean, a person is burning up with fever, you figure she's going to be in the hospital awhile, and you're wondering if her HMO is going to take care of this.

"Oh yes, certainly," Annie said. Her teeth were chattering. I was holding her in my arms. "Whenever I go away, I leave instructions with Sally Jean."

"Who's Sally Jean?" Maggie asked.

"My closest friend. You remember, don't you? The UN translator?"

"Is she in Maine now?"

"No, I don't know where she is just now. She moves around a lot. But she takes care of my HMO bills whenever they come in."

"How does she do that?" I asked.

"She sends them the money."

"How?" Maggie asked. "Cash? Credit card?"

"We have an arrangement," Annie said. "My health insurance is in perfect order. Don't worry, I'll give the hospital this little card I carry in my wallet."

When we got to the hospital and while Annie was being wheeled into the emergency room, Maggie asked me, "Did you ever meet this Sally Jean?"

"No. But Annie's mentioned her before. They used to room together in Amsterdam."

"So how come she pays Annie's bills for her?"

"She used to do translations for the UN."

"What kind of non sequitur is *that?*" Maggie asked, and kissed me on the cheek.

Our internist arrived a half-hour later, examined my sister, and asked at once if she had recently been in any country where she might have contracted malaria. Well, it so happened that the last country

Annie had visited (and this was where she also ate yams and shat in the woods) was one that announced in big signs at the airport MALARIA IS ENDEMIC IN PAPUA NEW GUINEA.

I don't know how Dr. Ernst knew at once that malaria was what Annie had. But upon questioning her further, it became apparent that not only did she *have* it, she also *knew* she had it.

"It comes and goes," she told him. "The high fever, the shakes."

Maggie and I stood by silently, listening. I was thinking, She *knew* she had malaria. She knew *before* she called from Maine. She came to us *knowing* she had malaria.

"How long have you been aware of these symptoms?" Dr. Ernst asked.

"Ever since I got back to the States."

"And when was that?"

"In April."

"You've had the symptoms regularly?"

"Well, on and off. I thought what it might be . . . you see, some fellow religious pilgrims and I . . ."

"Pilgrims?"

"I'm a Tantric adept," she said. "In Papua New Guinea, I hooked up with some other followers of the religion, and we were singing and chanting in the jungle one night, in the dark, and it was a marvelous and wonderful experience, transporting, in fact. So when I developed a fever a few weeks later, I thought it was due to this very high level of consciousness we'd achieved. This absorption into the cosmic weave."

Dr. Ernst looked baffled.

"Are you attributing *malaria* to some inspirational *religious* experience?" he asked.

Annie merely smiled at him as if she alone, and perhaps her guru, knew all the secrets of the universe.

"Why didn't you check yourself into a hospital in Maine?" Dr. Ernst asked her. "If you knew you were sick . . ."

"Actually, I'm afraid of hospitals," she said. "I don't like medication."

"Well, Miss," Dr. Ernst said, "you're in a hospital now, and I'm pre-scribing medication, and you had damn well better take it if you know what's good for you!"

Annie looked surprised.

In the corridor outside, Dr. Ernst said to me, "Your sister seems rather childish, doesn't she?"

❑

On her second day in the hospital, when the quinine had brought her fever down, and she was no longer shaking, I told Annie that the hospital wanted to know how she planned to pay her bills, and asked if I could have the HMO card she carried in her wallet.

Annie looked at me.

"The thing is," she said, "Sally Jean and I had a parting of the ways before I left for India. So she probably let the insurance lapse while I was gone."

"I thought she was your closest friend."

"Yes, she is. It's just that she comes and goes a lot."

"So what are you saying? You don't have medical insurance?"

"You know I don't trust the health care system."

"Yes, I know that. But you're in a hospital now, Annie . . ."

"Yes, Andy, thank you for informing me of that fact. I never would have guessed otherwise."

"So how do you expect to pay for your stay here?"

"I thought you said you were going to take care of me."

"I didn't mean . . ."

"You said, 'Don't worry, Annie, I'll take care of you.' "

"You were running a temperature of a hundred and . . ."

"It's what you said."

"I meant I'd get you to a *hospital*."

"Where *I'm* supposed to pick up the bills, right? I have a little jew-elry shop in Maine, you expect me to . . ."

"Annie, please, there's no need to get upset about this. Just tell them

141

you don't have health insurance and can't afford to pay for your stay here. They can't kick you out, you're a sick person. That's against the Hippocratic Oath. Okay?"

"Sure," she said. "Okay."

❑

When I went to the hospital the next morning, she was dressed in street clothes and sitting in a chair beside her bed, her face grim, her hands folded in her lap.

"What are you doing out of bed?" I asked.

"I'm leaving the hospital."

"Why?" I said.

"Because you won't pay my bills."

"I can't pay your bills, Annie. I can hardly afford to pay my *own* bills."

"Oh, poor little school teacher," she said.

"Don't mock me, Annie."

"Anyway, I don't have to stay here. I'm cured already."

"You're not cured. Dr. Ernst says . . ."

"What does Dr. Ernst know?"

"His specialty is infectious diseases."

"I don't have an infectious disease."

"You have malaria."

"If I had malaria, it's gone now. I don't have any fever . . ."

"Malaria hides. That's why you . . ."

"Hides?"

"Dr. Ernst says it hides."

"From whom?" she asked, and grinned at me slyly.

"A characteristic of the disease is that the parasite *hides*. You can think it's gone, but it isn't. That's why you have to take the medication for the full course. That's what Dr. Ernst says."

"Where's Dr. Tannenbaum?"

"Who's Dr. Tann . . . ? Annie, Dr. Tannenbaum was our family doctor. We haven't seen him in almost seven years!"

"He'd tell them to discharge me, all right."

"I doubt that very much."

"Oh yeah? I'm telling you he'd have me out of here in five minutes flat."

"He's probably dead by now. In any case, Dr. Ernst feels you should stay in the hospital until he's sure they . . ."

"Dr. Ernst isn't my doctor. Anyway, if nobody's going to pay my bills, why would they *want* me to stay?"

"I don't know what they do in cases like yours," I said. "I *do* know they . . ."

"What do you mean cases like mine?" she asked, and suddenly sat bolt upright. "What's that supposed to mean, cases like mine?"

"Cases where the patient is incapable of . . ."

"Incompetent?"

"Incapable. Of paying your own bills, is what I was trying to say."

"You said *you'd* pay my bills!"

"Annie, I said nothing of the sort."

"You said you'd take care of me!"

"That's right, I took you to the hospital . . ."

"What good is taking me to the hospital if you won't pay my bills!"

"Annie, I can't get into debt to a goddamn hospital!"

"Oh, but I can, right?"

"They'll make some arrangement with you, I'm sure. They have ways of dealing with people who don't have health insurance. I've already told them I'm not responsible for your bills."

"You went back on your word, is what you mean."

"I never said I'd . . ."

"You promise me one thing, and then you do another."

"I did *not* promise . . ."

"You think I don't know how much school teachers make?"

"A fortune, I'm sure. The point is . . ."

"Sure, joke about it. You always joke about it when it gets serious."

"The point is I never said I'd pay your bills, and I'm not responsible for them now. I can't stop you from leaving the hospital if you want to . . ."

"Damn right you can't."

"But if you want my advice . . ."

"Shove your advice."

" . . . you'll stay here till they're sure they've got all the bugs."

"I'm not staying here. I'm waiting for my discharge papers right this minute. You think I'm going to stay in a place that's charging me a fortune for giving me medication I never asked for?"

"You were burning alive with fever and shaking yourself to death. Annie, what the hell is wrong with you? Can't you see . . . ?"

"Oh, now there's something wrong with me. *You* break your word, so there's something wrong with *me*."

"Look," I said, "if you want to check out, check out. I can't stop . . ."

"Fine, asshole," she said. "Just go fuck yourself, okay?"

I stood there speechless, and then I nodded, and turned, and walked out of the room without saying goodbye. I did not begin crying until I was in the corridor outside. A woman was standing by the elevators down the hall. I turned away from her, and dried my eyes and my face with a clean white handkerchief. When the elevator arrived, I let the woman precede me into it. I looked off once down the corridor toward Annie's room. Then I stepped into the car, and the doors closed.

When I told Maggie what had happened, she said, "Why didn't you take her to a psychiatrist when I asked you to?"

"Because I really felt you were overreacting."

"No, it's because you didn't want to hear she was sick, Andy."

"That wasn't it. Don't you think I'd help Annie if I thought she needed help? I'd be the very *first* person to . . ."

"No, you'd be the very *last* person."

"She's my *twin,* Maggie. Of course I'd . . ."

"That's right."

" . . . help her. I'd do anything in my power to help her."

"Your twin, yes," Maggie said. "You're afraid that if *she's* nuts, *you* may be nuts, too."

"No, Maggie, that's not it," I said.

"Then what is it, Andy?"

"That's not it," I said again.

❑

By the summer of 1991, my mother had almost succeeded in murdering the Connecticut house. She never had it painted, never took care of any problems with running toilets or leaky roofs, never replaced broken or cracked flagstones in the walk leading to the front door, never patched gutters or leaders, allowed weeds to overcome and finally overthrow what had once been a vast green lawn, permitted yellow jackets to infest the turrets and gables, never had the chimneys cleaned or the trees pruned, just stood back from the house as if enjoying its slow and inevitable demise, as if watching my father himself dying in its stead. And when at last one night my father's studio did in fact collapse to the ground in a horrendous thunder storm that almost destroyed the main house as well, she put the property on the market, and would have been content to sell it for a third of what it might have been worth had she lovingly nurtured it over the years.

By that summer, my mother could no longer convince any prospective New York renters that the house was worth occupying even on a week-to-week basis. When she invited Maggie and me up for the weekend, we were frankly surprised. We didn't know she was even using the house anymore. But it was a sweltering day in the city, so we packed a bag, and caught an eleven-oh-five train from Grand Central, and were in Connecticut shortly after noon. A taxi dropped us at the house at twenty to one. My mother was already in a bathing suit.

"Hello, hello," she said, "how was the ride up?"

"Easy," I said, and took her hands, and kissed her on both cheeks. "Are we going to the beach?"

"Later."

"Not me," Maggie said. "Not today."

"Come," my mother said. "I have a surprise for you."

The surprise was Annie.

I had not seen her since that day in the hospital, almost seven months ago, when she'd memorably advised me to go fuck myself. I wasn't sure I was too tickled to see her now. She was wearing pink shorts and a purple tube-top blouse, her blond hair pulled to the back of her head in a pony tail, her face still festooned with all her little silver rings. Except for the ornaments, she looked much the way she'd looked when we were growing up together in this house, barefoot and sun-tanned, a big bashful grin on her face as she came down the steps from the porch, and opened her arms wide to me, and said, "I'm sorry, bro, forgive me."

I hugged her close.

Maggie stood apart, watching us.

"*Will* you forgive me?" Annie asked. "Please? I don't know what got into me, Andy, I really don't. I never use such language, you know I don't. I guess it was just the trauma of learning I had malaria, of all things . . . I mean, who gets malaria these days? And then discovering Sally Jean had let my HMO lapse like that, how could she have been so irresponsible? Please forgive me, Andy. Pretty please?"

"Twenty lashes," I said. "Bread and water for a week."

Annie laughed and hugged me close again, and then took my hands in both of hers, and held me at arms' length and said, "Let me look at you. Have you put on weight?"

"Just a few pounds."

"You should make sure he watches his diet, Magg."

"You're looking well," Maggie said.

"Thanks," my sister said. "Clean Maine living, you should come up sometime."

My mother was standing by, listening to all this apprehensively, pleased now that Annie and I seemed to have put our differences behind us.

"So who's for the beach?" she asked.

"I'm not a beach person," Annie said.

"I just got my period," Maggie said.

"Thank you for sharing that, darling," my mother said. "Looks like you and me, Andrew. Are you game?"

❏

The way Maggie later tells the story, my mother had left some white wine in the fridge and some sandwiches on the kitchen table. The women carry those out to the back of the house, and are sitting on the lawn, eating, drinking, chatting, when Annie mentions that she plans to take another trip sometime soon, for parts as yet unknown . . .

"I'm still doing research, in fact," she says. "I thought I might go back to Sweden. The people there are very tolerant of religions not in the mainstream."

"I've never been there," Maggie says.

"You should go sometime. You'd enjoy it."

"Will Sally Jean be going with you?"

"I haven't seen Sally Jean for months now," Annie says. "We had quite an argument, you know, about her letting my insurance lapse. She claimed she made all the payments when they came due, tried to put the blame on the company, can you believe it? I knew she was lying, she's such a damn liar. I mean, it was bad enough I had to be in a hospital, the things I know about the health care system. But to have them doubt my *word?* To have them *suspect* me that way?"

"Suspect you what way?" Maggie asks.

"Oh, you know. Thinking I was trying to pull a fast one. Like get free health care or something. They were probably told to keep a special eye on me. Dr. Ernst probably told them I'd 'attributed malaria to some inspirational *religious* experience,' were his exact words, mocking me like that."

"When did you plan to go?" Maggie asks, getting off the subject of hospitals; everyone in the family knows how Annie feels about the health care system.

"Oh, I don't know. The shop in Maine isn't doing too well, you know. And I don't have many friends up there, to tell the truth. I had a lot of friends in Sweden. That's where I first *met* Sally Jean, in fact, well, never mind her. I'll tell you, Maggie, I hope I never see her again. She's to blame for all my problems."

"Well, the hospital's behind you now, Annie. The main thing is that they were able to cure you. You haven't had any relapses, have you? No chills? No fever?"

"No, I'm fine. But . . ."

"So really, you should . . ."

"But I'm not talking about the *hospital,* don't get me started on hospitals. Anyway, who knows if I'm *really* cured? Who knows what kind of drugs they gave me in there? Ever since they linked me to her in Amsterdam, when we were rooming together, they won't leave me alone. They think I may have had something to do with those translations she made for the Russians. When there was still the cold war, do you remember?"

"Yes," Maggie says, "I remember."

"They just can't get it in their heads that I had nothing to do with it! They keep coming around in their damn blue jackets, I really feel I should call someone about it, their harassment. But who can I call? If they can reach someone like Dr. Ernst, I mean who knows how far their influence extends? Their control?"

Bees are buzzing in the clover. It is a hot, quiet, lazy afternoon. Maggie has no idea how close she is to treading dangerous ground. She hesitates a moment, and then, tentatively, she says, "You know, Annie, have you ever thought about discussing this with someone?"

"Discussing what with someone?"

"These people who follow you around and . . ."

"I *am* discussing it with someone. I'm discussing it with you."

"I meant someone qualified," Maggie says.

Annie looks at her.

"Maybe you ought to talk to someone before you leave the country again."

Annie keeps looking at her. Then, all at once, she nods, and gets up, and goes into the house. Maggie thinks she is going inside to pee. She is gone some three or four minutes, just enough time to find what she wants in the kitchen drawer. When Maggie turns again, she sees Annie coming at her with a claw hammer raised high above her head. The next thing she knows, it is crashing down on her left shoulder. She thinks Annie will hit her again, but instead she just yells, "Go fuck yourself, asshole!" and hurls the hammer onto the grass, and runs out of the yard.

Maggie sits alone on the lawn, stunned, her shoulder bruised and throbbing. She is still sitting outside when my mother and I return from the beach at a little past four, but she is now holding a towel full of ice cubes to her shoulder.

"What's wrong?" I ask at once.

"Annie hit me with a hammer," she says.

"Don't be ridiculous," my mother says.

"Mom, she hit me with a fucking hammer!"

"And I don't appreciate that language."

"Gee, I'm terribly sorry, but that's what your daughter did."

"Let me see that," I say.

"It's all swollen," Maggie says, sounding very much like a little girl. She lifts the towel for a moment. Her shoulder is a puffy mass of discolored flesh, blues and reds blending into purples. "There's the hammer," she says, and gives an angry toss of her head to indicate where it is still lying in the grass.

"Where's Annie?" my mother says.

"She left."

"Left?"

"She hit me and ran off."

"She didn't hit you, don't be silly," my mother says. "Where is she?"

"Is *everyone* in this family crazy?" Maggie asks. "I'm telling you she hit me with a hammer, and you're telling me I *dreamt* it?"

"Is she in the house?" my mother asks, and turns on her heel and immediately walks toward the porch and into the house.

"Call the police," Maggie tells me.

"No, I don't want to call the police."

"Andy, she *attacked* me!"

"I'd better go find her," I say, and start for the car. "Mom!"

My mother comes rushing out of the house.

"She's not here," she says. "What'd you say to her?"

"Mom, where are the . . . ?"

"What did *I* say . . ."

" . . . car keys?"

" . . . to *her?* How about what *she* said to *me?*"

"What'd you do to provoke her?"

"She called me an asshole! She told me to go fuck myself!"

"My daughter doesn't use such language. And she's not a violent person. You must have provoked her in some way. I'll go with you," my mother says, and we both start for the car.

"Andy!" Maggie calls.

My mother hands me the keys and throws open the door on the passenger side. I turn to where my wife is sitting with the towel pressed to her shoulder.

"Andy," she says very softly, "your sister hit me with a hammer. You should have her committed."

"No, I can't do that," I say, and get into the car, and insert the ignition key, and twist it. The engine roars into life. Maggie is still sitting there when I back the car out of the driveway.

My mother and I search all the back roads for the next two hours, but we cannot find Annie.

Annie is gone again.

When we get back to the house, so is Maggie.

❑

150

It is three minutes past eight when she arrives at Volumes and Tomes. I am standing outside the shop waiting for her. She is wearing this morning a dark blue pleated skirt, sheer blue pantyhose, black French-heeled pumps, a white blouse with a stock tie, and a gray jacket. She reminds me of the private-school girls you see walking along Madison Avenue on their way to or from school. The gray jacket is lacking only a school crest to make what she's wearing look like a uniform.

Maggie is a quite beautiful woman. When I first met her, I thought she was the most beautiful—but you already know that. Back then, she wore her black hair long to the shoulders . . . well, like a raven helmet. She now wears it cut much shorter. Her brown eyes are so dark they almost match her hair exactly. She wears no lipstick these days. I gather she considers this a "bookish" look. We greet each other perfunctorily. We do not even shake hands. It is strange that two people who made such passionate love together—at least in the beginning—cannot even shake hands in greeting anymore.

"To what do I owe the honor?" she asks.

"Annie's gone again," I tell her.

"So what else is new?"

"She may be schizophrenic," I say.

Maggie looks at me.

"She was hospitalized in Sicily. They diagnosed her as schizophrenic. She hears voices, Magg."

She keeps looking at me.

"What do you want from me?" she asks.

"I have to talk to someone."

"Why me?"

"You're the only one I know."

❑

It starts over coffee, it ends over coffee.

"You're looking well," Maggie says.

In all the years I was married to her, I never found the courage to correct her grammar. She is an educated person, a bookseller no less, and I am a teacher of English. But she still says, "You're looking well" instead of "You're looking good," and she still says, "I feel badly about this" instead of "I feel bad about this." When we were married, I used to wince at these grammatical lapses. We are no longer married. I no longer care if she uses "Between you and I" for "Between you and me." That was the worst of her assaults on the English language, and she used it with supreme confidence and maddening regularity. But I no longer care. I no longer care about her at all. That is the sadness of it.

"Thank you," I say. "And so are you."

She nods. Makes a slight moue. The facial expression says either "I know you're being nice," or "I know I look tired," or simply "Who cares what you think anymore?" which would put us on an equal footing. It is so sad. It is so fucking sad, really.

"So what's this about Sicily?" she asks.

I tell her what happened there. I tell her the doctor in Sicily thought Annie was schizophrenic . . .

"Thought?"

"Well, apparently she told him she hears voices."

"Apparently?"

"Well, I don't know what his credentials are, actually."

"But he's a doctor, isn't he?"

"A psychiatrist, yes. Presumably."

"Presumably," she repeats.

"Annie denies all of this, you realize."

"Mm. So you went to Sicily, huh?"

"Yes. To pick her up."

"The good brother," Maggie says.

There is an edge to her voice. For the longest time now, there has been a note of bitterness, or sarcasm, or even controlled anger whenever we discuss Annie. All at once, I wish we weren't sitting here together. All at once, I feel this is a huge mistake.

"Get you something?" a waitress asks.

"Just coffee," Maggie says.

"Coffee and a toasted English," I say.

The waitress pads off toward the counter. The shop is relatively quiet at this hour of the morning. On the avenue outside, there are men on their way to work, wearing suits and carrying dispatch cases, Soccer Moms who have just dropped the kiddies off at school, some of them in exercise clothes they will later wear to the gym, nibbling their lips, worrying. Everybody in this city worries. Especially since the attack, everyone worries.

"So how was Sicily?"

"I didn't see much of it."

"I always wanted to go to Sicily," she says almost wistfully. She shrugs, shakes her head, is silent for a moment. "So when did Annie vanish?" she asks.

I do not like her use of the word "vanish."

"My mother discovered her missing at two this morning. She went to see a psychiatrist here in New York last week . . ."

"A psychiatrist?" she says, surprised. She knows how my sister feels about the health care system.

"Yes. I took her to see a woman named Sarah Lang."

"The good brother," Maggie says again. "So you think this woman may have frightened her away, is that it?"

"I don't know what caused it this time," I say.

"Or *any* time," Maggie corrects.

"Two coffees," the waitress says, "a toasted English." She puts our order on the table, takes two packets of Equal from her pocket, sets those down as well, asks, "Anything else?" and, when she receives no response, goes back to the counter again. Maggie lifts her cup. She sips at the coffee. It is too hot. She purses her lips as if scalded. I suddenly remember that she cannot abide her coffee too hot. I suddenly remember this.

I remember, too . . .

And this comes back to me as if rolling on a loop of film which I can stop at will, frame after frame rolling past some hidden gate in some secret projector, flashing suddenly on the screen of my mind . . .

153

I remember driving through Massachusetts with Maggie.

She is wearing a pink blouse, a white summer skirt, sandals. Her knees are propped against the dash board, the skirt falling back onto her thighs. The windows are wide open, her long black hair is blowing in the wind. She is sipping coffee from a cardboard container.

We are on the way to her mother's house.

There are mountains on either side of the highway.

Maggie is going home.

She turns to me suddenly. There is a little girl's grin on her face.

"Nice, huh?" she says.

Grinning over the coffee container.

Nice, huh?

Yes, I think now. It was nice, Maggie. Sometimes it was nice.

She adds milk to her coffee cup, sips at it again, testing it. She looks across the table at me. Her dark brown eyes are very wide.

"I still don't know why you're here," she says.

"I want to apologize."

"Ah."

"I should have called the police that day."

"Yes, I think you should have."

"Maybe we could have helped her."

"I don't know about that, but it sure as hell wouldn't have hurt our marriage."

"I'm sorry, Magg."

"Yes, well, easy come, easy go," she says, and turns her head away, her eyes avoiding mine.

We are silent for several moments.

"Did you ever hear Annie talking to herself?"

"No."

"Not that day?"

"Never."

"Aaron thinks she does."

"Thinks?"

"Well, knows. He says this black girl . . . well, she must be a woman by now . . . Pearl Williams, she used to play keyboard in Annie's band. Aaron says she witnessed an incident . . . well, an episode, I guess, you'd call it . . . in Georgia. There would seem to be no . . . well . . . doubt . . . that Annie hears voices."

Maggie says nothing. She is staring at me across the table now.

"But you still don't quite believe it, do you, Andy?"

"I believe it," I say. "I think she may hear voices, yes."

"May."

"I guess she hears voices."

"You guess."

"I *know* she hears voices, all right? I think they may have spoken to her this time. I think that's why she's gone. Because they told her to leave. I don't know, Maggie. I don't know *what* the fuck these voices tell her or don't tell her!"

The waitress turns to us. She seems ready to come to the table, ready to ask us to leave if we can't maintain at least some small measure of decorum here. I want to tell her Hey, lady, my sister is a lunatic who may be about to harm herself or others, so what do you expect here, the New York Public Library?

"How do you know they spoke to her this time?" Maggie asks.

"My mother heard her talking to them."

"Saying what, exactly?"

"Mumbling. Nothing coherent. I think she might have been talking to the television set."

"That doesn't sound good, Andy."

"I know. What should I do, Magg?"

"I don't know how to advise you."

"I just want to help her, Magg. I don't know how to help her."

"Poor Andy," she says.

It seems for a moment that she will reach across the table to take my hand. She does not. It occurs to me that she will never again take my hand. Ever. I don't know why that should bother me so much. We've been divorced for almost ten years now. I don't know why that should bother me now.

155

"You should have believed me," she says.

"I should have."

"You should have cherished me more."

"I did cherish you, Magg."

"Ah, but not enough, not enough."

We sit there across the table from each other.

She sips at her coffee again.

Nice, huh?

I want to tell her that once I loved her very much. Once I adored her. I want to tell her that I don't know what went wrong with us, but something did, and it's a terrible dreadful shame, but I did love you, Magg, a whole lot. I loved you to death.

"I just want you to know there's never been anyone else but you, Magg. I don't know what went wrong with us, but there's never been another woman. I just want you to know that."

"Andy," she says, "there's been another woman for as long as I've known you."

And before I can ask her what the hell she's talking about, she says, "Your sister."

❑

We part on the sidewalk outside, like strangers. Like strangers, we do not even shake hands. She walks off in her direction, I in mine. There was a time when we would turn to look back at each other, the way lovers do. Mimed to each other. Folded our arms across our chests, opened them wide to say I love you, I love you. Once, twice, sometimes three or four times before we lost sight of each other. There was a time.

I do not turn to watch her now.

I feel certain she is not watching me, either.

I start up First Avenue, toward Twenty-third. I'll catch a crosstown bus there, and then connect to an uptown subway on Broadway. It is a bright clear morning in New York. This is still only August, but there is the promise of September in the air. I am wearing gray slacks and a tropical weight blue blazer. I am wearing a white shirt open at the throat, and gray socks, and black loafers. Normally, in August, during school vacation, I wear jeans and a T-shirt all day long. But today, my sister is gone, and I do not know to which police detective or hospital official I may soon be speaking. I am not dressed formally, but I am dressed respectably, for whatever encounter with bureaucracy may lie ahead.

I do not want to go back to my mother's apartment. I do not want to sit there with a family that has been lying to me for the past sixteen years. I do not want to revisit the human debris there. The clutter here in the streets is by contrast tumultuous and rich with life. I walk unseen among lovers and tourists, children and their grandparents, pets on leashes. I can remember mornings and afternoons in this city with my mother and Annie, the pair of us larking ahead of her on the sidewalk, my mother walking proudly behind us.

Where did we lose her?

Where has she gone this time?

I try to piece together the shattered fragments, the minuscule bits of mosaic that together form Annie's past. Is there something there that will lead me to where she is now? But she has never left a trail before, my sister. She is as secretive and as skilled at deception as any of the imaginary FBI agents she believes are pursuing—

It suddenly occurs to me that perhaps Annie *herself* is a secret agent!

I burst out laughing.

A woman walking past looks at me as if I'm crazy.

"Sorry," I say to her, and raise my eyebrows and pull a face and hunch my shoulders in apology.

But why not, actually?

Isn't it possible that Sven Lindqvist in Stockholm was the recruiter who enlisted her? She came back to the U.S. as a sleeper, only to be summoned abroad by him several months later when she received an urgent message to sell all our band equipment and rush back to Stockholm, where for the first time she was to meet her European counterpart, the infamous UN translator named Sally Jean. Sven has been her control ever since. It is Sven who sends her all over the world on secret assignments. It is Sven who brought together the team of surgeons who spirited her off that Air France flight and installed a radio transmitter in her skull or her rectum or wherever. It is Sven who sent her down to Greenwich Village that New Year's Eve to spy on the guys from Dartmouth and Harvard, two hotbeds of Communist activity. It is Sven who brought her back from India disguised as a Tantric adept in baggy pants and sandals with hennaed hair and a silver circlet over her right eye and lice that were probably radio transmitters in their own right. It is Sven, too, who arranged for the agent Wally Hennessy (ah-ha! A *booking* agent, or an *FBI* agent?) to send The Gutter Rats on a tour of the South, where Annie would contact her Georgian counterpart, Harley Welles, disguised as a redneck policeman, and henceforth exchange vital nuclear secrets hidden in her urine, which she generously sprayed all over Harley's uniform leg and polished black shoes while the black secret agent Pearl Williams stood by taking discreet notes. It is Sven who arranged for her to rendezvous once again with Sally Jean in Amsterdam, where she scattered broken glass around her bed and searched her bags for secrets.

It is Sven who kissed her only twice in the moonlight, but captured her mind forever.

All entirely plausible.

I am smiling now.

I don't care who thinks I'm crazy, I am smiling.

I walk in brilliant sunshine, smiling.

I do not want to go back to that apartment on Eighty-first Street, but I don't know where else to go, or what else to do.

And suddenly, I feel so utterly alone.

8

I had to learn how to be alone.

I was twenty-six years old when Maggie and I got divorced. The singles scene was alien to me. I didn't know where to go. I didn't know what to do with myself. I stayed home a lot. I read a lot. I considered quitting teaching and going to Paris, after all, but I knew I'd never been any good at writing, knew I'd just be kidding myself all over again. I felt suddenly old. My wife was gone, and my sister was gone, and I felt like one of those old men you see on flaking green benches in the park, feeding the pigeons, tossing peanuts to the pigeons.

My sister claims she was in Tiananmen Square on June 3, 1989. I know she was in Asia at that time because I got married in September of that year, and she wasn't there for the wedding. She wasn't there for the divorce, either. She would have been almost twenty-three when Maggie and I got married, which is when she took her second trip to India, which expanded into her sojourn in Nepal and then China, and then

Papua New Guinea. But whether or not she was in Tiananmen Square on the day the tanks opened fire is a matter of conjecture. In light of recent events, as they say, I doubt everything she has ever told me.

And yet, she was remarkably knowledgeable about the events of that day and the days preceding it, and the internal politics of Deng's regime, which caused him to force the resignation of Hu Yaobang, his popular right hand man—well, she always was a good student.

She says she was at the Xidan intersection when the soldiers opened fire on a crowd of Chinese trying to block them. She says she ran with the others, trying to hide. She says the soldiers kept firing, even after no one was trying to bar their way.

"One minute, it was like a country fair in the heart of a huge city, the people cheering the students, the students cheering the people, and the next thing you knew there were machine guns firing. The agents spoke fluent Mandarin, you know, they were well-trained. I could see them running in and out of the demonstrators, egging them on."

"What agents?" I asked.

Even then, I wanted to know what agents.

"The ones who incited the riots," she told me.

She did not say they were FBI agents. I could easily have believed she was talking about Deng's own people.

She told me all this while we were sitting on the roof of the building my mother still lives in on Eighty-first and West End. No pigeons on this rooftop. Only ramparts and parapets, the hum of traffic far below, Annie telling me that despite what the world was led to believe by those pictures of the lone student bravely holding off a column of four tanks, what actually happened was that the tanks ran over *anyone* who stood in their path.

"Even after the army reclaimed the square, the tanks kept roaming the streets, firing on people. Soldiers were firing their weapons in the air. There was blood everywhere. Everywhere." The sun was low on the horizon now. We loved to watch the setting sun. "There were no pigeons in the square," she told me. "The Chinese kill birds, you know. They won't let them rest. They chase them whenever they land. They keep them flying in the air until they get exhausted from flapping their wings, and fall to the ground dead." The rooftop towers were in silhouette now; Manhattan could very well have been Camelot, all ablaze with red as bold as blood. "Do you remember the funny names all the geese had?" she asked. "In the book?"

"Oh yes," I said.

"Ank and Wink-Wink . . ."

"And Lyo-lyok . . ."

"I liked her best."

"Remember Aahng-ung the glutton?"

"And Ky-yow . . ."

"And Lyow the singer?"

"Such funny names."

"So long ago," I said.

"Flying across the North Sea, do you remember that?"

" '*Bump*—they were on the ground,' " I quoted.

My sister picked up on it at once, finishing the passage for me. " 'They held their wings above their heads for a moment,' " she said, " 'then folded them with a quick and pretty neatness.' "

And together we shouted, " 'They had crossed the North Sea!' " and burst out laughing.

"Oh such fun!" Annie said.

"Oh such language!" I said.

But now there are no pigeons in Tiananmen Square.

❑

The last time I saw Annie before her trip to Italy was in February of this year. I went up to Maine for the weekend of the twenty-second. On the car radio, they were talking about the Olympics in Salt Lake City. The Russians were now demanding a duplicate gold medal for their skater, Irina Slutskaya, who they said had beaten sixteen-year-old Sarah Hughes . . .

"Why not give *everyone* a gold medal?" I asked the radio.

At the Hague, Slobodan Milosevic had projected for the Tribunal judges a documentary movie made by an American film maker, attempting to prove that all his crimes should be blamed on anyone but himself.

"Fat Chance Department," I said, and began stabbing at buttons on the dash, trying to find a station playing classical music, a near impossibility on the road. By chance, I stumbled upon public radio, but it came in riddled with static. I finally settled for a station playing pop and advertising merchants in Portland.

In this, the dead of our American winter, I drove up Maine's craggy shoreline to visit my sister for the last time before she left for Europe and who knew where else? The landscape was desolate. What during the summer must have been festive seaside resorts were now shuttered and windblown hot dog stands, large brooding hotels, and Ferris wheels with their empty gaily painted seats rocking in the wind. I drove the rented car with the heater up full, and even then I was shivering.

My mother had told me that Annie was living in "a charming seaside cottage."

I drove up a gravel driveway lined with scraggly bushes and withered stalks of weeds. A wooden shack with gray smoke billowing from its brick chimney sat on the edge of a cliff, the sky beyond it menacing and forlorn. Below, huge waves crashed against a narrow beach strewn with shiny black rocks. Salt spray burst on the brittle air.

I parked the car as close to the house as I could. Struggling against the wind, I took my small suitcase from the trunk, carried it to the front door, and knocked.

I had not seen my sister for several months now.

I had only my mother's reports to go on.

I think I mentioned that Annie usually takes very good care of herself. She is a tall woman with a stately carriage and blond hair she normally wears falling loose and sleek to her shoulders. She rarely wears makeup . . . well, she doesn't need any, really. Her green eyes are somewhat almond shaped, and she has thick lashes, and high cheekbones, and a good nose, and a full mouth that makes its statement without benefit of lipstick, truly. She has always been a quite beautiful girl.

I did not recognize the woman who opened the door for me.

"Andy?" she said. "*Hey,* bro!"

And took me in her arms, and hugged me.

She was wearing what my mother used to call "a candy-store owner" sweater, a shapeless gray cardigan missing several buttons down its front, hanging open over the sort of housedress my grandmother Rozalia used to wear when she was cleaning the house in New Rochelle, a loose-fitting cotton garment printed with a vague flower design on a faded green field. Her hair was clipped short. It framed her face haphazardly and appeared grimy and limp, as if she hadn't washed it in days or even weeks. She was wearing combat boots with leather laces, and cotton stockings of a sort of buff color, wrinkled and hanging limp on her legs, distorting the shape of them and adding to the impression of . . . well . . . a shopping bag lady who'd just come back from searching through garbage cans on a city street. She had gained weight, but she did not appear plump, she merely looked . . . unhealthy. Unkempt and unhealthy.

"How are you, Sis?" I asked.

"Oh, fine, Andy, just fine," she said. "Let me look at you." Holding my hands, she held me at arms' length and studied me approvingly, nodding, smiling. "Your hands are *freezing,*" she said, "come sit by the fire, come. Would you like some tea? I just made some wonderful herbal tea, a friend of mine sells organic food in a little shop she owns, you'll meet her tonight, would you like some?"

"Yes, I'd love some."

She had replaced the ring in her left nostril with one of her own design. It strongly resembled a miniature silver penis, its eye decorated with a tiny red ruby, as if its bulbous head were bleeding. The circlet over her right eye was similarly fashioned of silver. It was etched with miniature markings of what I supposed was Sanskrit.

I sat by the fire in a chair upholstered in cracked and peeling brown leather. It looked like something a lawyer might have thrown out when he was redecorating his office, something Annie might have found in some back alley someplace.

"How was the drive up?" she asked.

"Fine. Cold. Barren. But fine."

"Oooo, yes, it's cold up here. I can't wait to get out."

She was at the stove now, in the small kitchen that formed part of this . . . well . . . this *dump* she was living in. Mama's "charming sea-side cottage" was in fact a single large room with four double-hung windows and walls papered with peeling wallpaper in a repeating pink hibiscus pattern that seemed more suited to Florida than to Maine. One corner of the room had been set aside as a work space, with a high stool and a table upon which Annie had spread her tools and her works in progress. In the kitchen, there was a chipped white enamel-topped table, with two wooden chairs painted green around it. There was a single bed on one wall of the room, and a cot on the other, both of them covered with fringed throws that looked Indian, and an unpainted dresser with an incense burner and a cluster of candles of various sizes on its top, and there was a clothes line hanging near the fireplace, festooned now with woolen—well, *bloomers,* I have to call them, because they were too shapeless to be called panties—of the same buff color as Annie's stockings. All at once, I got the feeling that my sister was living at the poverty level. All at once, I wondered exactly how much money my mother was sending her each month.

"Did you want lemon or milk in this?" she asked.

"Lemon, please," I said.

"Good, because I ran out of milk this morning."

She brought me the tea in a mug. "Here," she said, "drink this while it's hot," and handed me the mug and a paper napkin. I opened the napkin and spread it on my lap. I warmed my hands on the steaming mug.

"Taste it," she said.

I sipped at the tea.

"Nice, huh?" she said.

"Mm, delicious."

"I told you," she said, smiling.

She sat opposite me on a low stool, tucking the faded housedress between her legs. The fire crackled and spit.

"When are you leaving?" I asked.

"The sooner the better," she said.

"Yes, but when?"

"I thought the middle of March. Italy's no great shakes in February, you know. I thought I'd get there just as spring arrives."

"Good timing," I said.

"Oh sure."

"Where will you be going first?" I asked.

"Sicily, I think. It's all the way to the south. It should be nice and warm there in March."

"But you don't know yet."

"No, not yet. Well, I have time. I'm trying to get a cheap ticket on a charter flight. You know Mom."

"Where will you be staying?"

"Oh, I'll find a place, don't worry. I always do."

"I wish you'd keep in touch this time."

"I'll call you, sure."

"You promise?"

"I promise. You want to see what I've been making? I think the jewelry's taking some new and very exciting turns, really. I'm so happy with it. Come," she said, "let me show you," and took my hand and pulled me out of the easy chair so suddenly that I spilled tea getting up.

"Ooops!" I said, and started dabbing with the paper napkin.

"Leave that," Annie said, "I'll get it later. Come."

Her jewelry seemed to have become amorphous somehow, almost misshapen. She proudly exhibited rings that resembled mangled male organs, pins that were presumably vaginas but appeared more like runny eggs, earrings that seemed too spiky and even dangerous to wear.

"Beautiful, huh?"

"She said modestly."

165

"Well, don't you think so?" she asked.

"Gorgeous, yes."

"Come *on!*" she said, and punched me playfully on the arm. "I worked hard on this stuff."

"It's beautiful," I said. "Truly."

But it wasn't.

❑

We met her friends for dinner at seven-thirty that Saturday night. The place Annie chose was a Thai restaurant on the edge of a marsh. Wide windows framed tufted brown stalks lighted from spots mounted on the building's roof. The menu was moderately priced, but I had the feeling that Annie and her friends considered the place elegant. All of them behaved as if dining out was a rare occurrence, a treat to be savored, and remembered, and perhaps cherished. There was certainly a holiday atmosphere around the table as we settled in and ordered drinks. I began to feel relaxed for the first time since I'd left New York.

Jessie Kilgallen was the woman who ran the organic food store. Some thirty-eight years old, dressed for the climate in jeans, a bulky blue turtleneck sweater, and a woolen ski cap and padded blue parka, neither of which she removed. The restaurant was, in fact, a bit chilly. Everything in Maine, in February, seemed a bit chilly.

Buck Crowley was in his mid-forties, I guessed, a broad-shouldered man with a gruff and hearty manner and a ruddy complexion that hinted at a great deal of time spent outdoors. He was wearing a bristly reddish-brown mustache and sporting a red plaid woolen shirt and wide red suspenders. He snapped one of the suspenders and asked, "Why do firemen wear red suspenders?"

"Oh God, not that one," Jessie said.

"Why *do* firemen wear red suspenders?" I asked dutifully.

"To hold up their pants," he said, and Jessie rolled her eyes.

Buck was not a fireman. He was, instead, a painter—I now noticed the traces of paint on his fingers and under his fingernails—who'd been living here in Maine for the past almost ten years, since right after the Gulf War, where he'd served in the First Infantry Division.

"I drove an M1-A1 Abrams tank equipped with a plow," he said. "Our job was to cut lanes through a ten-mile-wide stretch of barbed wire, minefields, bunkers, and trenches north of the Iraqi–Saudi Arabian border. This was in February of '91," he said. "The war was almost over."

"Buck was a war hero," Annie said.

"Some hero," Jessie said. "He buried people alive in their trenches."

"We bulldozed the trenches so the ragheads wouldn't use them for cover," Buck said. "It saved a lot of hand to hand fighting. You know, Jess, a lot of you bleeding heart individuals . . ."

"Oh, that's me, all right," Jessie said, "a bleeding heart individual."

"A lot of you have the notion that burying guys alive is nastier than blowing them up with hand grenades or sticking them in the gut with bayonets. Well, it's not."

"I'm sure I'd prefer being buried alive, you're right," Jessie said.

"We killed maybe a thousand of the cocksuckers," Buck said.

The word caused Jessie to raise her eyebrows, but she made no comment otherwise. Neither did Annie. Our drinks came. Buck had ordered a vodka martini straight up, "a pair of olives, please." I had ordered Johnnie Walker Black, on the rocks. The two women had ordered Chardonnay. We toasted Annie's imminent trip abroad . . .

"Safe journey, hon," Buck said.

"Sweet dreams," Jessie said.

"Come home soon," I said.

And we drank.

A waiter brought us menus.

"The secret of Thai cooking," Annie said, "is in . . ."

"She knows the secrets of the entire universe," Jessie said.

"I *do* happen to know Thai cooking," Annie said. "The secret is in harmonizing the four primary flavors."

"She's a very *good* cook, in fact," Buck said, as though confiding something confidential to me. I had the feeling he was trying to tell me he'd been sleeping with my sister.

"Salty, sweet, spicy, and sour," Annie said. "Or bitter, if you want to add a fifth flavor, but that's not essential."

"The question is what should we *eat?*" Jessie said, tapping the menu and grinning at me as if she'd just made a joke to rival the one about the red suspenders.

"It's like the primary colors in painting," Buck said.

"I didn't know there were four primary colors," Jessie said.

"Well, no, just three. But it's the same thing. It's a matter of balance."

"That's it *exactly,*" Annie said. "So here's what I'd suggest, if you'd care for my expert opinion."

"Annie Gulliver, Expert," Jessie said.

We started with a hot and sour shrimp soup, and then my sister ordered something that turned out to be beef fried with hot pepper, garlic, and sweet basil. She also ordered fresh broccoli fried in garlic and oyster sauce, and chicken cooked in coconut milk with lemon grass and galanga . . .

"It's called *kha* in Thailand," my sister said.

. . . and half a dozen tasty little deep-fried spring rolls . . .

"I'll burst!" Jessie said, and rolled her eyes.

. . . and a salted, steamed, and fried mackerel, served with a lime-juice dip and a paste made of shrimp, pepper, and garlic.

Buck stayed with his martinis, but I ordered a full bottle of Chardonnay, and poured for my sister and Jessie, and then for myself. We toasted again, this time to celebrate the news that Buck's work would be exhibited in a Kennebunkport gallery this coming summer.

"The secret of great art . . ." he started to say, and Jessie said, "Another expert here," and grinned at me again. I wondered if she was coming on. I wondered if Annie had told her she had a divorced and available twin brother. She wasn't at all bad-looking, a trim woman with short brownish hair now that she'd taken off the woolen hat, and perky breasts in a tight sweater, visible now that she'd removed the parka.

"The secret of great art," Buck repeated, "is how the artist maintains tension in his canvas. I like . . ."

"Or *hers*," Jessie corrected.

"I like my paintings to tug at the canvas from each corner."

He started to demonstrate this with his huge hands, and Jessie warned, "*Watch* it, you'll knock over the wine!" and reached for the bottle, almost knocking it over herself.

"The first thing I ask myself is 'How can I make this painting inaccessible?' " Buck said.

"The Great Communicator," Jessie said, which I thought was somewhat comical.

"Where are you from originally?" I asked her.

"New Jersey," she said.

"Anywhere near Ridley Hills?"

"Never heard of it."

"It's near Princeton."

"She never heard of Princeton, either," Buck said.

I had the feeling he was trying to tell me he'd been to bed with Jessie, too. I suddenly wondered if the three of them had been to bed together. I suddenly remembered that my sister was a Tantric adept. I suddenly remembered that there were four enjoyments in the Tantric religious ceremony, the last of which was intercourse with a stranger.

"So how'd you end up here in Maine?" I asked Jessie.

"I'm into health," she said. "Not health *care*," she added quickly and spread her hands wide to my sister, as if to ward off an impending blow. Buck laughed. My sister didn't. Neither did I. I had the feeling both Annie's friends were familiar with her views on health care, and had teased her about it in the past. "I'm an organic farmer," Jessie said. "I grow all the food I sell in my shop. No pesticides, no herbicides, no commercial fertilizers. Just good clean natural ingredients."

"She's got a compost heap a mile high in her back yard," Buck said.

"Grass clippings, weeds, garden and kitchen waste, animal manures . . ."

"Please, not while I'm eating," Buck said.

"I enjoy selling food that's grown in healthy, vibrant soil. I enjoy breathing air that isn't polluted," Jessie said. "I enjoy . . ."

"She enjoys fucking in the outdoors," Buck said.

"As if you would know," Jessie said.

"As if anyone would *care* to know," Annie said. "Who wants dessert?"

We ordered fried bananas and vanilla ice cream.

"How big is your store?" I asked Jessie.

"It's just a little hole in the wall," Buck answered.

"About as big as your gallery in Kennebunkport," Jessie said.

"It's not *my* gallery," Buck said.

"And it's a nice gallery," Annie said. "Small, but nice."

"Will this be a one-man show?" I asked.

"No, just one of my paintings," Buck said.

"Tugging at the canvas from all four corners," Jessie said.

"Well, it's a small gallery, and I paint big," Buck explained.

"My father paints big, too," I said. "He's a painter, you know."

"He knows," Annie said.

"I know. Big famous *artist,* I know," Buck said. "I heard it a hundred times."

"It happens to be true," I said.

"Oh, sure."

"He *is* a big famous artist. He's Terrence Gulliver."

"Sure, I know."

"The show in Kennebunkport is for six area artists," Annie said. "It's difficult for emerging artists here in Maine, you know."

"It's difficult for emerging artists *anywhere,*" Buck said.

"At least you can breathe fresh air here," Jessie said.

"Well, there are other places that have fresh air," Annie said. "Where you don't have to be harassed all the time."

"Who's harassing you, hon?" Buck asked.

"Forget it," Annie said.

"No, seriously. I'll go talk to them."

"He'll go bury them alive in their trenches."

"Just some people who came by the shop," Annie said. "I have to show you the shop, Andy. It's really very cute."

"What people?" Buck insisted.

"The Indecency Police," Annie said, and pulled a face. "People who have certain opinions about what constitutes high art, and what doesn't."

"Maybe you shouldn't make dirty jewelry," Jessie said. "Am I the only one who finds these bananas a little too sweet?"

Annie was looking at her.

"*What?*" Jessie said, meeting her eyes dead on.

It looked for a moment as if my sister would burst into tears. Instead she only shook her head.

"Maybe *you* shouldn't sell food grown in pig shit," I told Jessie.

Buck laughed.

Jessie gave me a look that said You want to fuck me or insult me, which?

"I had a long drive today," I said. "Let me get the check."

❑

Annie's shop was at the northern end of a strip mall directly on US 1. The plows had been through early that Sunday morning, but the snow heaped on either side of the highway was already turning a sooty gray from the steady stream of traffic in either direction. The shop itself was pencil-thin, a narrow sliver wedged between a barbecue joint on one side and a discount shoe store on the other. The lettering on the plate glass window of her shop read ANNIE'S JEWELRY. A small display in the window exhibited some of her less explicit pieces.

She unlocked the door and flicked a switch. Fluorescent light filled the small, cramped space. Easing herself behind a narrow display case, she slid open one of the glass panels, and then laid out several pieces on a black velvet pad.

"These are some of the latest ones," she said.

I was looking at an array of formless, unstructured, vaguely erotic pieces done in silver and copper. But I had learned my lesson well.

"They're beautiful," I said.

"Aren't they?" Annie said, smiling.

"So what's this about the Indecency Police?"

"Please," she said. "Don't get me started."

"Is that what they call themselves?"

"No, that's what *I* call them. But that's what they are, all right. This self-appointed group determined to stifle any form of creativity that isn't absolutely orthodox."

Her breath was pluming out of her mouth as she spoke. I realized that the shop was frighteningly cold, and wondered if she could afford to heat it during the daytime.

"They actually came by to see you?"

"Oh, on more than one occasion. Two men and a woman. The first time, they pretended to be interested in my jewelry. But I was onto them the second time. The third time, they became actually threatening."

"What do you mean, threatening?"

"Oh, making all sorts of veiled threats, you know how these people are."

"Well, did you call the police?"

"What good would that have done? You think it's only *here* this is happening? It's all over America. That's the main reason I want to get out of here. Look at what happened in New York. Remember that big imbroglio at the Brooklyn Museum of Art, where I forget the painter's name, he put a clump of elephant dung on the breast of a black Madonna, and there were cutouts of genitalia in the background— *Chris* something his name was, this black kid from London? Well, the Indecency Police felt this was an insult to Christianity or whatever, and threatened to cut off financing to the museum, that's the way they get you, you know, they cut off financing. They don't *need* a reason to close you down, they just come and *do* it!"

"But, Annie, they *didn't* close it down. In fact, the exhibit was very successful. Besides, why would anyone . . . honey, can we get out of here, please? I'm freezing to death."

"I thought you'd never ask," she said, and grinned like a little girl.

❑

The shack seemed almost cozy.

Annie started a good fire the moment we got home, and we sat in front of it, drinking her good herbal tea, and talking again about her impending trip, which really seemed to excite her.

"I hear that Lu might be in Italy this summer . . ."

"Lou? Who's that, Annie?"

"Lu. L-U. He's a teacher of Buddhist Tantra yoga, don't you *read* anything, bro? Sheng-yen Lu? The Grand Master? Doesn't that name mean anything to you? I don't know where he'll be yet, or even *if*, he may be dead for all I know. But that's what I heard. And wow, would I love to hear him speak! Can you imagine!"

"Do you think you'll get on a charter flight?"

"Oh, yeah, there are plenty of them, don't worry."

"Annie . . . is Mama sending you enough money?"

"Oh sure."

"How much does she send you?"

"Why do you want to know?"

"I don't like to think you're . . . wanting for anything."

"No, I'm fine. She sends me enough. Really."

"How much?"

"A thousand a month. I can get by really well on that in Italy."

"Because . . . if that's not enough . . ."

"It's *plenty*, bro. What *is* this?"

"I was thinking . . . maybe I could help out."

173

"Come on, you're a *school* teacher."

"I could maybe send you three, four hundred dollars a month," I said. "If you think that'd help."

"I don't need it, Andy, really. It'll be cheap in Italy," she said. "I'll be fine, really."

"You sure?"

"I'm positive. But thanks, you're very sweet."

She reached over, took my hands in hers.

"I adore you, you know," she said.

"I adore you, too," I said.

"No," she said, and shook her head, and looked up into my face. "I *really* adore you."

"Good. So take care of yourself, okay?"

"I will, don't worry."

"Promise me."

"I promise."

"Don't get into trouble with any Indecency Patrols."

"Police. And that's not their real name, I told you. That's just the name I gave them. Do you want some more tea?"

"Yes, please. What *is* their real name?"

"How should I know?" Annie asked, and got up and went to the stove. "Do secret organizations tell *you* their real names?"

"I don't *know* any secret organizations, Annie."

"That's exactly my point."

"What I'm asking . . . why would they go after somebody who makes jewelry?"

"Well, these are *art* pieces, you know."

"I realize that. But why would they consider your work a threat?"

"Who knows?" she said, and handed me the fresh mug of tea. "Why was elephant shit considered a threat? I'm a menace to their conservative values. Well, look at it, Andy. I have a two-by-four shop in a strip mall in the asshole of creation, and they're coming after me. Ask yourself why."

"I already asked you why, Annie."

"And I'm *telling* you why. Don't be so dense."

"Well," I said, and took a sip of the tea. It was very hot. We were silent for several moments. The clock on the fireplace mantel ticked noisily. Outside, I could hear the ocean crashing in against the rocks.

"What's with Jessie and Buck?" I asked.

"What do you want to know?"

"They seem like losers."

"They are."

"So why do you hang around with them?"

"Not for long, kiddo."

"Why are you hanging around with them *now?*"

"I'm not. I thought you might like company for dinner, that's all. Thought you might like to meet some genuine Maine types," she said, and grinned.

"I came up to see *you*, Annie. Not some woman who shoots you down all night long . . ."

"Oh, I'm aware of that, don't worry."

"And some jackass who calls Dad a 'big famous *artist,*' I wanted to punch him right in the mouth!"

"He's jealous is all. His paintings stink. He's a loser, like you said. Look, Andy, don't you think I'm onto them?"

"Then why'd you invite them to dinner? Why'd you turn the other cheek every time they . . . ?"

"I know exactly how to deal with such people, don't worry. The minute I know someone's out to get me . . ."

"Out to *get* you? They're two piss-poor . . ."

"Didn't you hear all that sexual innuendo? They think Tantra is an excuse for promiscuity, but it isn't that at all. Jessie's an anachronistic hippie who's been to bed with every dirt farmer in Maine. Who knows *what* Buck was involved in over there with his tank burying people? All these macho warlords are closet fags, you know, don't you read the papers? They abduct twelve-year-olds from the marketplace, you can't even go out to buy an orange! Please, don't get me started, Andy. Buck and Jessie are the main reason I'm getting *out* of here!"

175

"You don't have to go all the way to Sicily to end a relationship, Annie."

"Oh no? Where else can an artist go to work in peace, without everyone telling her what to do? You think I enjoy the constant spying and ridicule?"

"I'm sure there are art communities . . ."

"Not in America, don't kid yourself. No one in this country is willing to give an emerging artist a break! No one! They come around in skintight pants, you can see their genitals and everything, and they stand outside your shop window and slit their throats with their fingers, how are you supposed to work in that kind of threatening climate?"

"Annie, you're remembering wrong. That happened in England."

"It happened here, too, don't kid yourself. I can't wait to get out." She was silent for a moment.

Then she asked, "Do you think I'll ever be as good as Dad?"

"Well, you're working in two different mediums," I said.

"Oh, I know. I meant comparatively. He's very good, you know."

"I know, Annie."

"I loved him so much," she said.

❏

I left Maine the next day after lunch.

Annie and I stood on the rockbound shore, hugging each other, saying our goodbyes. The wind was sharp, the sky was clear.

The next time I saw her would be in the mental ward of a hospital in Sicily.

9

The moment I step into the apartment, my mother asks, "Where were you?"

"I went to see Maggie."

"Why on earth did you . . . ?"

"To apologize. You might want to do the same thing, Mom."

"I have no need to apologize to your former wife."

"Annie hit her with a hammer," I remind her.

"What!" Aaron says.

"Annie did no such thing."

"Okay, Mom, fine. Let's just keep pretending Annie is the girl next door, okay? Let's just keep doing what we've been doing all along, pretending Annie isn't sick, allowing *her* to believe she isn't sick . . ."

"That's right, she isn't."

"Yes, but she *is,* damn it! We should have got help for her right after Georgia."

"Georgia," she says, and waves it aside. "That was almost comical."

"It wasn't comical, Mom."

"Urinating on a cop? I think that's comical," she says, and tries a laugh that dies abruptly in her throat because all at once she sees the dead serious expression on my face, and knows I'm not here to provoke laughter, kiddies, you can count on that.

"She was talking to people who weren't there," I say. "That isn't comical, Mom."

"According to that black girl, yes," my mother says. "A drug addict."

"She wasn't a drug addict, Mom," Aaron says.

"Who knows what drugs they were using, your sister and her so-called musician friends."

"Mom, she was hallucinating," I say. "First she thought a waitress was spying . . ."

"What waitress? Aaron didn't tell me about any waitress. What's this got to do with the fire house? Sometimes I think you're as . . ."

She cuts herself short.

"What waitress?" she asks.

"In Atlanta. Annie slapped a newspaper out of her hands and then shoved her off a stool."

"Why didn't you tell me this, Aaron?"

"I did, Mom."

"I don't remember anything about a waitress. Why would Annie attack a waitress? She's not a violent person."

"Mom, she hit Maggie with . . ."

"If we're to believe Maggie."

"Yes, well, I believe her."

"If you believe her so much, you shouldn't have divorced her."

"Mom, I think Annie is a danger to herself and to others. I think we should call the police."

"No."

"Yes, before she . . ."

"We should have called them seventeen years ago," Augusta says. My mother turns to her, puzzled.

"When she stole the thousand bucks from us."

"That is a lie!"

"It's the truth, Mom," Aaron says. "Kelly saw her taking the money."

"*Kelly*," my mother says, dismissing her.

"My daughter, Mom."

"Your *daughter*," she says, dismissing her yet again. "You bring me two grandchildren from . . ."

She shakes her head.

"Never mind," she says.

"No, let's hear it," Augusta says. "Two grandchildren from *where*, Mom?"

"From who *knows* where? Instead of . . ." She cuts herself off again. "Never mind," she says again.

"Instead of *what*, Mom?" Aaron asks. "Instead of having two kids who might turn out to be nuts?"

"I do *not* have . . ."

"I'm talking about the twins Augusta was carrying. This was after Georgia, we knew all about Georgia. Do you know what the odds would have been?"

"I don't want to hear odds, save your odds."

"If either of your parents has schizophrenia, your chances of getting it are ten percent," Aaron says.

"Oh? Do you and Augusta have schizophrenia?"

"Mom, we knew Annie was nuts! The odds on . . ."

"Enough with the odds!" my mother says. "What time does the first race start?"

"She doesn't believe anything we say," Augusta says. "What's the use, Aaron?"

"That's right, Miss, what's the use? I don't believe my daughter stole money from you, and I don't believe she went after Margaret with a hammer, either. Margaret tripped and fell, that's how she got the bruise."

"I'm calling the police," I say, and start for the phone table.

"You want them to lock her up, is that it? You want them to lock up a person who's as sane as you or I? My daughter has never in her life tried to hurt anyone."

"She hit Maggie with a hammer," I say, more evenly this time, stressing each word.

"No, she did not. Margaret probably fell. They'd been drinking wine, she probably . . ."

"No, Mother, Annie hit her with a fucking *hammer!*"

"Don't you *dare* use that language in my house!" my mother yells, and for a moment I fear she will slap me, but instead she clenches both hands, and turns away from me. I watch her silent struggle for control. She is trembling with rage, her knuckles white where she presses her hands together, her thin shoulders shaking. All at once, she seems so very small and slight. I almost want to take her in my arms and comfort her. She shakes her head, as if suspecting I might try to embrace her, and warding off any such motion beforehand.

"If you all want to believe Annie's crazy, fine," she says, "believe it. But I don't think it's wrong for a mother to help and encourage her own daughter . . ."

"You haven't helped her," I say.

"I've done everything I know how . . ."

"You've enabled her, is what you've done. She needs real help." My mother is shaking her head. I am talking to a stone wall. "Mom, she hears *voices!*" I say. "She talks to *voices.* You said so yourself."

"I said she was murmuring, mumbling, whatever. That's what people do when they're thinking out loud. What's so terrible about that? Don't you ever think out loud?"

"No, never, Mom."

"Never," Augusta says.

"Don't you ever talk to yourself?"

"Never."

"Well, I do."

"That's not the same as hearing things."

"Hearing things is just another way of saying talking to yourself. You talk things over with yourself. You pose a question, you answer it. That's not so unusual. Everybody does it."

"I don't," Augusta says.

"I don't, either."

"Inside your *head* is what I'm saying. Even if Annie *did* hear someone talking to her, that doesn't make her crazy. She heard a voice, she talked back to it. That isn't so unusual you know. I don't know why you're making such a big deal of it. If Annie ran away, it wasn't because any voices told her to. It's only because I wouldn't give her the money."

"What money?" I ask at once. "What are you talking about?"

"The fifty thousand dollars."

"Fifty . . ."

"It's my fault she's gone," my mother says. "I told her to leave."

"What!"

"I told her to go, I told her to get out."

"Oh, Jesus, Mom."

"Don't look at me that way! Do you know what living with her is like? *You* try it sometime! *You* try living with a goddamn *lunatic!*" she shouts, and suddenly she is in tears. "You try . . . you try . . ." she stammers, and then collapses onto the sofa again, and covers her face with her hands. "I'm sorry," she says, "oh dear God, I'm so sorry. I should have given her the money, oh please God, let her be all right, I was only trying to help. But it . . . it . . . I didn't know what to do. I just . . . didn't know what to do anymore. All at once, it . . . it got to be . . . too much for me . . . all at once. I . . . just couldn't bear it any longer. You don't know what it was like. You don't know what it was like."

Aaron sits beside her and puts his arm around her.

Weeping into his shoulder, she tells us what it was like.

❏

At first, she thinks Annie is really okay.

Really.

Before her "incarceration in Sicily," as Annie refers to it, she acquired a deep tan and is now in remarkable physical condition from walking and swimming . . .

"And falling down mountains," my mother adds jokingly, and Annie even finds this funny.

It would appear that whatever medication they prescribed for her in Italy has had a calming effect. She is truly a joy to be with. Truly. For the first time in a very long time, my mother feels as if she actually has a grown daughter with whom she can go shopping at Bloomie's or Bendel's, with whom she can visit the Met or the Modern, a daughter she can take to lunch at the Russian Tea Room or the Café des Artistes. Annie seems to have become once again the bright, articulate, inventive, charming individual Mama knew before she sold our band equipment and went to Sweden on her own.

It is Annie who helps her hang new drapes in the guest room, where she will now be sleeping and working. Together, chatting and reminiscing, they clear a corner of the room so that she can set up a work table. At first, because she is still feeling the effects of the drug they injected in Sicily, Annie sleeps a lot. But as the days go by, she spends more and more time on her jewelry, and my mother believes she truly has the makings of a good sculptor. When she's not at her table molding silver or copper or gold into these truly remarkable . . . well . . . works of art, she is either pacing the apartment thinking up new designs, or else sketching them onto a pad for later realization in metal.

My mother still doesn't quite know what happened in Sicily, but she doesn't believe that Annie experienced any sort of psychotic episode, and she certainly doesn't believe the diagnosis Bertuzzi made. She knows that except for a little marijuana as part of the Tantric cere-mony, Annie is not a drug-user, so she feels positive that narcotics were not responsible for the altercation in the bar. But she's beginning to re-alize that Annie can become aggravated at the slightest provocation. As an example, just the other night, she got into an argument with a waiter in a Spanish restaurant because he was unable to tell her what ingredi-ents were in several dishes on the menu. But was a similar lack of com-munication responsible for what happened in Sicily? Was the bar episode due to a language barrier? Similarly, were those toughs on the road really trying to rob her and rape her? Or were they just trying to frighten her? My mother has by now heard so many versions of the story, she just doesn't know.

Aside from that one outburst in the Spanish restaurant, however, Annie's been fine ever since she got home, helping with household chores, leaving her work space tidy and neat, and being a truly pleasant companion. My mother sometimes becomes dejected about Annie's misspent life and wasted prospects, but she honestly believes Annie's essentially a contented person with great talent and sincere convic-tions, and that's what my mother feels is important. In fact, she is de-lighted when Annie tells her she's managed to find a part-time job in a jewelry store in Brooklyn, and will begin work there on the Saturday after the Fourth.

My mother really thinks Annie is okay now.

Really.

But suddenly, all of that changes.

❑

As best I can figure it, Shirley's birthday party took place on the Sat-urday my sister started work in Brooklyn. This would have been the day after my mother and I had our summit meeting in the park. Shirley was my mother's best friend, and so the ladies were taking her to lunch at Le Cirque, an extravagance to be sure, but, hey, how often do you celebrate your sixty-fifth?

When my mother gets back to the apartment at around three that afternoon, Annie is watching television in the living room. My mother is surprised.

"Hi," she says. "What are you doing home so early?"

"Short day today," Annie says. "How was your party?"

"Oh, it was such fun," my mother says. "How's the job?"

"Fine. Too bad I wasn't invited."

"Well, it was just the girls," my mother says. "Tell me about it."

"Nothing to tell. It's a job."

"Can I turn this off, honey?"

"Sure."

My mother turns off the television set, and comes to sit beside Annie.

"Is he a nice man?"

"He's fine. Were any of the *other* daughters invited?"

"No. I told you. It was just . . ."

"Just the ladies who lunch, I know. Sondheim, Mom. Remember Sondheim? You were in *West Side Story,* remember, Mom? You ought to know Sondheim. You ought to know 'The Ladies Who Lunch.' "

"That wasn't in *West Side Story.*"

"Wherever it was."

"But yes, I *do* know Sondheim," my mother says. "Personally, in fact."

"The way I know Sheng-yen Lu personally," Annie says. "How'd Sondheim like your tiny feet?"

"I do have tiny feet."

"Yes, I know. I thought maybe some of the other daughters were invited."

"No."

"I thought maybe some of your friends invited daughters they aren't ashamed of."

"Annie!" my mother says. "Whatever gave you such an idea? I *adore* you, why would I be ashamed of you?"

"Maybe none of your friends have daughters who were locked up in Sicily."

"I wouldn't trade a dozen of them for you, darling," my mother says and pats her hand.

"I'll bet," Annie says. "How'd Shirley like that scarf you bought her?"

"Oh, she loved it. Well, anything Hermès, you know."

"I guess she doesn't wear jewelry, right?"

"Jewelry, too. *Hermès* jewelry, yes. She adores anything . . ."

"Any Gullivers in her collection?"

"Gulli . . . ?"

"Her vast collection of jewelry? Any pieces by the talented young Annie Gulliver?"

My mother looks at her.

"Oh, darling, I'm *so* sorry," she says, "forgive me. I never thought of it. Of course, I should have given her a piece of your work. How stupid of me. You should have suggested it, Annie. I'm sure she'd have loved it."

"Oh, I'll bet. The way you love it."

"I do love it. I think you're very talented, darling."

"Oh, yes, and your friends all have such wonderful taste, too, I know. How could Shirley *not* love a cunt pinned to her left breast?"

"Annie, *please!* I *hate* that kind of language."

"But you love my work, right? I can't *say* cunt, but it's perfectly all right for me to *sculpt* cunts!"

"Are you deliberately trying to offend me?"

"Far be it," Annie says, and puts her hands together as if in prayer, and bows her head to Mama. "But you just *might* have thought about giving Shirley a genuine work of art instead of something frivolous you picked up at Barney's or Saks . . ."

"Berg . . ."

"*Wherever* the fuck you bought it! The point is . . ."

"I said I was sorry."

"Apology accepted," Annie says, and the room goes silent.

"Can we get off this now?" my mother asks. "Please?"

"Sure. What'd you have for lunch?"

"Never mind lunch. What'd you mean a short day today? How could Saturday . . . ?"

"A short day for *me,* Mama."

My mother still looks puzzled.

"I quit, Mama."

"You quit? This was your first day on the job, how could you quit?"

"He was looking at me cockeyed."

"Who, Annie?"

"The owner of the shop."

"Cockeyed how?"

"Cockeyed. Like he didn't trust me or something."

"Thank God. I thought you meant he was some kind of rapist!"

"*All* men are predators, but this one kept watching me as if I was planning The Great Jewel Robbery. All his precious costume jewelry! A fat-ass jeweler in Brooklyn with the intelligence of a cockroach. I'll never go back there, never."

"Annie, you said it yourself. It's a job. A job is a job."

"I have a job. I make jewelry."

"And you'll sell it one day, I know you will. But meanwhile . . ."

"Not to you or your friends, that's for sure."

"Annie, how often must I apologize for . . . ?"

"Forget it, you apologized, right, I forgot."

"You just have to give it time, darling. But meanwhile, I think you should try to find a job you can hold for a while. You've never . . ."

"I didn't *want* to hold this job."

"Well, Annie, you've never held a job for more than a week. I don't see any difference between this time and all the other . . ."

"*Quitting* a job isn't the same thing as not being able to *hold* a job! I *quit* this job, Mom. I quit it because I was onto that fat bastard from the minute I walked into his shop. I knew he'd been warned about me beforehand, and I knew he was just waiting for me to make a false move so he could report me. Besides . . ."

"Report you? To whom? I thought he was the owner of the . . ."

"Besides, that's not the kind of work I want or need. I have my jewelry. I'm an artist. And to continue growing I have to keep improving my spiritual life. Trotting all the way out to Brooklyn is not my idea of spiritual enrichment!"

"That's all well and good, Annie, but everyone needs to eat."

"I'm not interested in material things, the way you and your ladies who lunch are, the way my fat brother Aaron is! I'm happy to work on my jewelry, to be able to commit to my religious beliefs through my jewelry. If you and your ladies who lunch . . ."

"Let me remind you," my mother says quite evenly, "that one of your so-called ladies who lunch is putting food in your belly and a roof over your head while you recuperate! I certainly don't expect gratitude, but the least you can . . ."

"For your information, I'm *fully* recuperated, Mama. I'm a happy and healthy person. In fact, I was never happier in my life than I was in Italy, when those bastards came along and fucked it all up. I'm not to blame for what others . . ."

"How can you say you're happy? You're almost thirty-six years old, and all you've got to your name is a pair of dirty socks with holes in them!"

"Hyperbole, Mama, hyperbole! Besides, I don't *need* material things! I'm an artist. I build spiritual communication with people who share my sensibilities and beliefs. These people are my true friends. They don't care if my socks have holes in them, who gives a shit about . . . ?"

"What friends? You don't *have* any friends, Annie, face it. You never stay anywhere long enough to *make* friends. If you got a steady job, maybe you'd . . ."

"I do have friends. Have you ever asked about this Serbian man I've been seeing, whose name is Mirko, and whose company I enjoy? He's an artist who's involved with Vedic astrology, he teaches English as a second language. His father was a successful architect. He fled from Belgrade seven years ago, do you even *care?*"

"I care deeply, Annie. But I'm not going to stand here and let you scream at me this way."

"Then go fuck yourself!" Annie says, and storms into her room, and locks the door.

❏

"She hasn't spoken to me for three days now," my mother tells Shirley.

They are having lunch in a Chinese restaurant on Broadway. Shirley is sporting the Hermès scarf Mama gave her for her birthday. She clucks her tongue in sympathy.

"What do you suppose she's angry about?"

"Everything," my mother says.

"Are you giving her money?"

"Right now, a hundred dollars a week. But while she was . . ."

"Helene, please! You're not impoverished, you know."

"That's just for spending money, just enough for her to get around the city."

"Even so."

"I was giving her a thousand a month while she was in Italy."

"That's not very much, either. No wonder she got in trouble."

"You think?"

"Absolutely. That's bare subsistence level, Helene. She was bound to meet sleazy people sooner or later."

"I just don't know what to do," my mother says. "I don't think she'll ever be able to earn a decent living making jewelry. I'd be willing to help her pay for reasonable housing in a modest neighborhood, but I feel she should . . . well, don't you think she should first show me that she can hold on to a paying job?"

"Oh yes. Absolutely."

"And learn how to socialize with others?"

"It's funny you should mention socializing."

"I mean, she hasn't *spoken* to me for the past three days."

"Maybe she stopped taking her medication," Shirley says. "That happens. They stop taking the medication, and they get . . . you know . . . withdrawn."

"Yes. Well. I just don't know. Andy's supposed to be meeting with her sometime this week, he's going to talk to her about seeing a psychiatrist. But I'm not even sure that's such a good idea. I just don't know what to do, Shirl. She's been living with me since early in July, and all at once I'm afraid of coming out of my own bedroom."

"What are you saying?"

"She scares me, Shirl. My own daughter."

My mother begins weeping. She takes a handkerchief from her bag, begins dabbing at her eyes.

"Helene?"

"Yes. I'm sorry, forgive me."

"Why don't you go see this social worker I was starting to tell you about? They have support groups, you know, where you can meet people whose relatives are having similar problems. I think it might help you, I honestly do."

"It's just . . . she's never behaved this way before."

"Well, what happened in Italy must have been traumatic."

"Even so."

"Take the card, call her. Let me know how it turns out."

"Thank you, Shirl." My mother looks at the card, puts it in her wallet. "She called us the ladies who lunch," she says.

"Well, we are," Shirley says, and picks up an egg roll.

❑

My mother still isn't sure.

For a few days—I calculate this to be the time just before our visit to Dr. Lang—Annie seems all right again. Not exactly the loving daughter

189

she'd been at the beginning of the month, but at least communicative and working on her jewelry again. And then, right after our visit to Dr. Lang, Annie once again stops talking to my mother. Mama decides that seeing a psychiatrist was a mistake to begin with.

Yesterday morning, while Annie is doing her mantras in the guest room, Mama calls the mental health association whose name is on the card Shirley gave her. She leaves a message saying, in effect, that she wants to talk to someone about a daughter who seems . . . well . . . extremely troubled.

At around two or two-thirty yesterday afternoon, my mother realizes she is out of milk and orange juice, and decides to go down to the market. Annie is watching an old black and white movie on television.

"Annie?" my mother says, "Do you want to come shopping with me?"

"No, thanks," Annie says. "Do you think she's smarter than I am?"

"Smarter? Joan Crawford?"

"Whatever her name is."

"No, not at all."

"They say she's smarter."

"In what way?"

"In *every* way. They think I'm stupid."

"Well, honey, she has these script writers, you know . . ."

"Forget it!" Annie snaps.

"Are you sure you don't want to come along?"

"Positive," Annie says, and then mutters something my mother can't quite make out.

"What?"

"Nothing," Annie says, and turns to the television set again, and listens to a line or two of dialogue, and then begins mumbling again.

"Are you all right?" my mother asks.

"I'm fine. Why? What's wrong?"

"Nothing," my mother says. "Honey, I'm expecting a call from California . . ."

"California? Who do you know in California?"

"A friend, you don't know her. Please don't answer the phone, okay? Just let it ring."

"What friend do you have in California?" Annie asks.

"I'll be back in fifteen, twenty minutes."

When my mother leaves the apartment, Annie is still mumbling to herself. This is very troubling to Mama. More troubling than we can possibly know. When she comes back half an hour later, Annie has turned off the television set and is sitting in a chair facing the door, her arms folded across her chest, her feet flat on the floor, her eyes glaring.

"What is it?" my mother asks.

"Did you call some mental health organization and tell them you have a mentally ill daughter?"

"No," my mother says.

"Some twerp just called and asked if I was the party who has a mentally ill relative."

"No, I never said anything like that. I told them I was trying to understand my daughter and wanted to join . . ."

"You called a mental *health* organization?"

"Yes. What's wrong with that?"

"What's wrong with *you*, you crazy bitch?"

The violence of her words is like a slap in the face. My mother actually backs away from her.

"You obsessed control freak! How *dare* you call me a mentally ill person?"

"But I *didn't,* Annie."

"You're supposed to love me so fucking much, you tell some twerp I'm mentally *ill?* You want the truth? You're not interested in truly loving anyone, all you want is to control people!"

"Annie, you know that isn't . . ."

"And when you can't accomplish that, you become angry and bitter and you go around making irresponsible and reckless statements about your own daughter's mental stability!"

"Annie, for God's sake . . ."

"That's why none of your children will have anything to do with you! Aaron moved to New Jersey, Andy can't keep a marriage going because he's got a mother who suffers from separation anxiety disorder, do you know what that is? Of course you don't, they never know! And now you betray the only person who's shown the slightest bit of compassion for you!"

"I'm sorry if someone said something stupid to you on the phone, but believe me . . ."

"Oh, yes, go ahead, go through your usual routine of rage and self-pity, tell me how truly, very, very sorry . . ."

"I *am* sorry, Annie. But . . ."

"You have some big emotional problems, Mommie Dearest. That's why all your children consider you a threat to their happiness. Do you care at all about any of us? Do you care at all about *me?* Do you care at all about Mirko?"

"Mir . . . ?"

"My Serbian friend! See? You've already forgotten all about him."

"I'm sorry, Annie. I had no idea you'd found someone who . . ."

"Oh, stop it, will you, please? I'm not about to *marry* the man, so stop counting grandchildren on all your fingers and toes. Just tell me what the fuck you plan to *do!* I will not accept any more of your fanatical belief that I am not a sane person!"

"What would you *like* me to do, Annie?"

"Give me my stipend."

"What stipend?"

"My fifty thousand dollars."

"I don't know what fif . . ."

"The stipend I'm entitled to, no strings attached, a genuine gesture of trust and good faith."

"I can't give you fifty thousand dollars, Annie."

"Gee, what a surprise! I have plenty of friends from wealthy families who are given large amounts of money to do whatever they want, with the parents' blessing and love. You give me a lousy hundred dollars a week, and you consider that a small fortune!"

"I'm sorry if you don't think that's enough, Annie . . ."

"No, it isn't enough, and you *know* it isn't!"

" . . . but I don't *have* fifty thousand dollars to give you."

"Then I'm leaving," Annie says.

My mother looks at her.

"So leave," she says.

"Sure, kick me out!" Annie yells. "You think I'm not wise to you? You give me money so you can control me. But when I refuse to do whatever you wish . . ."

"Go, Annie, okay?"

" . . . you cut off funds! That's your way of maintaining control, you think I don't know? There are control freaks like you riddling the entire health care system! *I'm* the relative who's mentally ill? You call to tell them you have a mentally ill *relative?* You're the crazy one, you controlling bitch!"

"Leave me alone, Annie. Go. Get out of here!"

"You think I don't know all about you? I know more about mental health than anyone in this family! Heal thyself, physician! Look into your own crazy head! Hear what they're telling you, madam!"

"Go!" my mother screams. "Get out, get *out,* just *go!*"

❑

"She waited till the middle of the night," my mother says now. "I could hear her pacing in her room, and then I thought she'd gone to sleep because I couldn't hear her anymore. But when I got up to go to the bathroom, I looked in on her, and she was gone. It's my fault. I told her to get out. Oh dear God, I told her to . . . please . . . just . . . *leave!*"

"It's all right, Mom, come on," Aaron says.

"No, it's *not* all right!" I say. "She was in crisis, and you kicked her out!"

"What do you know about any of this?" my mother shouts. "Go

193

talk to your little bookseller, you love her so much! Do you know what it was like, dealing with Annie all these years? I never knew whether I was talking to her or her goddamn *voices!*"

"What!" I say at once.

Augusta picks up on it, too. "What do you mean?" she says. "Did you . . . ?"

"You *knew* about her voices?"

"You all seem to think she hears voices . . ."

"No, Mom, *wait* a minute! When did you find out about her voices?"

"I didn't."

"You just said . . ."

"I didn't know about them."

"You said you didn't know who you were talking to . . ."

"Leave me alone!"

" . . . her or her goddamn *voices!* When did you find out about them, Mom?"

"She knew about them," Augusta tells Aaron.

"When, Mom?"

"I don't remember," she says.

"When was it, Mom?"

"I just told you I don't remember."

"Was it after she went to Sweden alone?"

"It could have been. I don't remember."

"Mom? Was that when Annie told you she was hearing voices?"

My mother says nothing.

"Mom?"

"Yes. When she got back from Sweden that time."

"She was only sixteen! If you'd tried to get help then . . ."

"*Stop* it!" she says. "I did everything I could! I told her it was not unusual for a person to hear voices when she was depressed. I told her she'd experienced with Sven the exact same thing I'd experienced with her father. And . . ."

"Sven was a teenage *crush!*"

"Yes, but he abandoned her the same way. And so we both experienced depression, and as a result . . ."

"Oh, Jesus, what are you saying, Mom? Did *you* hear voices, too?"

"Only because I was so depressed. I went to see a doctor. I was terrified. The voices were telling me to kill myself! I was thinking of *killing* myself!"

"It's all right, Mom," Aaron says.

"He told me hallucinations were a common symptom of depression. Your father had just *abandoned* me. The doctor told me it was perfectly all right for . . ."

"Perfectly all *right?*"

" . . . for a depressed person to hear voices. Eventually, they went away. But I was so scared, so scared. And then . . . life is funny. I suddenly had more important things to worry about than your father and his girlfriends. My mother had cancer."

"So you told Annie it was normal to hear voices."

"If a person was depressed."

"You told her it was fucking *normal!*"

"Don't tell *me* how I should have talked to my own daughter!" my mother shouts. "Were you the one hearing voices? Don't you think I *know* I'm responsible for the way she is? Don't you think I've blamed myself *enough* all these years?"

"You're not to blame, Mom," Aaron says at once, and takes her in his arms. "You *knew* something was wrong, so you went to see a doctor. Crazy people don't do that."

"Yes, she *is* to blame," I say.

And the telephone rings.

10

The piercing sound shatters the stillness of the room, paralyzing us. No one moves for the phone. We turn to look at the ringing instrument, but no one reaches for it.

"Well, is someone going to answer that?" my mother asks.

Augusta is standing closest to the telephone table. She picks up the receiver.

"Hello?" she says.

And then, again, "Hello?"

She puts the receiver back on its cradle.

"Nobody," she says.

"Annie!" I say at once. "Do you have caller ID, Mom?"

"No."

"Why wouldn't she talk to me?" Augusta asks, sounding hurt.

"Damn it, *I* should have picked up!"

"We didn't know it was Annie."

"We *still* don't know who it was," Aaron says.

"Who else would hang up?"

"At least we know she's okay."

"*If* it was her."

The phone rings again.

Augusta is reaching for it.

"Leave it!" I shout, and grab for the receiver after the second ring.

"Annie?" I say.

"Hey, bro," she says.

She sounds very tired, very far away.

"Where are you, honey?"

"Oh dear, where am I?" she says.

"Annie? Honey, tell me where you are."

"Oh, you know."

"No, I don't. Tell me, Annie. I'll come get you. We'll go have a cappuccino together."

"Oh nooooo, no more cappuccinos. I know you. You take a girl for a cappuccino, and next thing you know a psychiatrist is telling her she's crazy."

"Honey, where are you? Tell me, okay?"

"I'm someplace safe. Don't worry, Andy. You don't have to worry about me. I'm okay now."

"What's that noise I hear?"

"What noise? I don't hear any noise."

"That sound? What is it, Annie?"

"Let me talk to her," my mother says, and snatches the phone from my hand. "Annie?" she says. "Honey, I'm so sorry we argued yesterday, there was no need for that. I love you, Annie, I love you with all my heart. Please come home, and we'll work out some way to . . ." She looks at the receiver. "Annie?" she says. "Annie?" and turns to us, a surprised look on her face. "She's gone," she says, and gently replaces the phone on its cradle.

"What's her cell phone number?" I say. "You *must* have it someplace."

"I don't remember her giving it to me."

"*If* she gave it to you, where would it be?"

"In my book."

"Where's your book, Mom?"

"The desk there."

With a sideward dip of her head, she indicates a drop leaf desk on the wall just inside the entrance door. Aaron and I start for it in the same moment, almost colliding. We back off, and then start for the desk again. I reach it first. There is a small key in the drop leaf front. I twist the key, hold it to pull open the flap.

"Where, Mom?" Aaron asks.

"It should be there someplace."

"*Where?*" I shout, and the phone rings again.

"Don't anybody touch it!" I yell, and run across the room for it, the phone ringing twice, three times, I yank the receiver off the cradle.

"Annie?"

There is an instant's surprised silence.

Then a man's voice says, "May I speak to Helene Lederer, please?"

"Who's this?" I ask at once.

"My name is Jason. If you have a moment, I'd like to explain the advantages of the ultimate mileage card. Is this *Mr.* Lederer?"

"Goodbye," I tell him, and hang up. "If it rings again, please let me . . ."

The phone rings.

I snatch the receiver from its cradle.

"Hello?"

"Where'd you go, Andy?"

"Don't hang up, honey."

"Just don't put Mom on again, okay?" she says.

"I won't."

"Promise?"

"I promise. Where are you, Annie?"

"On my way to the North Sea," she says.

"Are you at an airport?"

"In a sense, bro, in a sense."

"What's that sound, Annie?"

"Beats me. Listen, I want to tell you something."

"Tell me."

"Do you remember when we thought a raccoon was breaking into the house? That was me, Andy."

"I know. You told me."

"I *did?* What a big-mouth, huh? I was watching the road for Daddy."

"I know."

"You think he's ever coming home, Andy?"

"I don't think so, hon."

"Does he really have another little girl?"

"I'm sure he doesn't. You're his little girl, Annie. Tell me where you are, and I'll come get you."

"You don't have to worry, I'm okay."

"I just miss you, hon. Tell me where you are."

"Just don't worry about me, okay?"

"Annie . . . is that the wind I hear?"

"I don't know what you're hearing, Andy. I'd better go now," she says abruptly, and hangs up.

Aaron sees the look on my face.

"What?" he says.

"I know where she is," I say.

"Where?"

"I'll be back," I say, and start for the front door.

"Let me come with you."

I turn to him. My hand is already on the door knob.

"I'd better go alone, Aaron."

Our eyes meet.

Aaron nods.

"Good luck, bro," he says.

I open the door and step out into the hall. Behind me, I hear my mother say, "Don't call the police!"

I close the door on her words, and walk swiftly to the elevators.

❏

There is more traffic in the streets than anyone might expect on a hot weekday in August, when most New Yorkers are at the beach or in the mountains. And though I keep urging the turbaned Sikh cabbie to please step on it, his dark-eyed gaze meets mine implacably in the rear-view mirror. He drops me off on the northeast corner of Columbus and Seventy-second. I turn the corner and hurry eastward, toward the park. There is a dry cleaning establishment that wasn't there sixteen years ago. There is also a deli I don't remember. The candy store seems familiar but I do not recognize the Korean man behind the counter.

The building we lived in for so many years stands like a white-brick fortress between two shorter red-brick buildings that flank it like bookends. A green awning with the address on it in white stretches toward the curb. There was no uniformed doorman when we were living there. Neither is there one now. There is, instead, a short sturdy man in his sixties, wearing jeans and high-topped workman's shoes, and a blue denim shirt with the sleeves rolled up to his forearms.

The years have been kind to Mr. Alvarez.

His complexion is smooth and his dark eyes sparkle, and the mustache under his nose is neatly trimmed. He turns as I approach the building, smiles, asks, "Help you, sir?" and then recognizes me. "Andrew?" he says. "Andrew?" and holds both hands out to me. I take his hands. Grinning, he keeps staring into my face. "How are you, Andrew?" he asks. His accent is as thick as it was when I was a boy growing up. "Are you looking for your sister?"

"Yes. Is she here?"

"She got here about an hour ago. I let her go up the roof to see the pigeons. Is that okay?"

"Sure, thank you, Mr. Alvarez."

I am thinking she was wandering the city all night long. She just got here an hour ago. I am thinking I may not be too late.

"Is she all right, Andrew?"

I hesitate for a moment.

Then I say, "No, Mr. Alvarez, she's very sick. Can you please call the police for me, tell them to send an ambulance? I'll be on the roof with her."

"She works for the FBI now, your sister?"

"No," I say, and rush into the lobby toward the elevator bank. I push the button, and the doors slide open. I move into the car, press the button for twenty-three.

"Is your father still painting?" Mr. Alvarez asks.

But before I can answer, the doors close.

❏

The big metal fire door to the roof is closed, but not locked. I twist the knob, and shove the door open, and come out onto a tarred roof that is blisteringly hot in the noonday sun. I turn automatically and at once toward the pigeon coops on the right. The birds huddle on their perches, cooing softly, gently rustling their wings.

Annie is sitting on the floor of the roof, in the shade of the pigeon coops, her back to them, her arms around her knees, her head bent. She is wearing a light chiffon shift that riffles in the breeze. Her hair is blowing around her face. Twenty-four stories below, I can hear the rush of traffic, the incessant murmur of the city. I walk to her swiftly.

"Annie?" I say.

She looks up.

"Hi," she says. "Which one is Lyo-lyok? I looked at all the geese, but I couldn't tell which one she is, they all look the same to me now. None of them have identities anymore."

"I don't think she's here, honey."

"Oh, sure, she is. She's going to fly me to the North Sea."

"I don't think so, honey. Come on, let's go home." I say, and reach for her hand.

"*No!*" she shouts, and recoils from me, her eyes wide.

"It's me, honey," I say. "You don't have to . . ."

"I *know* who it is, don't tell me who it *is*."

She squints at me, brushes hair out of her eyes.

"So you found me, huh?" she says. "You knew where to find me."

"I heard the pigeons."

"I knew you'd figure it out. Did you tell Mama where I am?"

"No, I didn't."

"Don't tell her."

"I won't."

"She'll call them again."

"Don't worry."

"Do you know what she did?" she asks, and turns to me, her eyes wide. "She called some twerp at a so-called *health* facility, and told her I'm mentally *ill,* can you believe it? That's another way of stealing a person's identity, you know. They declare you mentally ill, and bingo, they steal your identity! It's a very sophisticated way of controlling a person. Once you own a person's identity, you control that person, you see. It's like getting raped. If you rape a person, you own that person for the rest of your life. Because you've violated her mind and her body. It's all about control, it's all about identity. If you can't keep your own identity, what's the use? That's why I had to get out of there, Andy. Because Mama called them, and they were onto me."

"I didn't tell her where you are, honey."

"She's crazy, you know. She hears voices. She told me she hears voices. Can you believe it? She looks just like a regular person, doesn't she? But Morgan le Fay used to be able to assume different forms, too, you know. Do you remember when Kay and the Wart first met her? Lying on a bed of lard, that was so *funny!* She wasn't beautiful at all, just this big fat slob lying in all that lard, ick! Mama's a messenger of the Great Oppression, you know, come to abolish the Tantric religion. I was warned by my guru," she says, and looks directly into my face.

Her eyes are wide.

I think of Archimedes the owl. I remember my father reading to us. I remember the little girl who was my precious sister, Annie.

"Fire comes out of Mama's mouth," she whispers, "did you know that? She told me it was my fault Daddy left, because he didn't want so many children, and she wouldn't let him smoke in the living room. He wasn't expecting *two* of us, you see, he didn't know there'd be twins. So he told her to get rid of me, and when she wouldn't he left with his bimbo, is what she told me. But smoke was pouring out of her mouth when she said it, so I knew it wasn't true. Well, you've seen the smoke, you know what it's like."

I sit beside her.

She does not try to move away.

Together, we sit in the shade, our backs to the coops.

"No one holds my hand anymore," she says.

I take her hand in mine.

"No one likes me," she says.

"I like you," I say.

"Well, you," she says, and smiles. "Dear Andy."

She puts her head on my shoulder.

She seems so tired.

We sit holding hands like children.

I can remember the two of us running in the park together, hand in hand. I can remember the two of us in school together, our hands popping up whenever a teacher asked a question. She was so smart, my sister. So beautiful. My twin. My dearest twin.

"Mama's such a liar," she says, shaking her head. "It wasn't *my* fault Daddy left, it was Sven's."

"Come on," I say, "let's go home. We'll worry about Mama later."

"No, Andy, we've got to worry about her *now*," she says earnestly. "She wants to put me in a strait jacket again. Have you ever been in a strait jacket, do you know what *that* feels like? If Daddy had known what they were doing to me, he'd've been there in a *minute!* He writes to me all the time, you know, we correspond regularly when I'm abroad. He told me all about why he left, never mind *Mama's* story. The minute he found out what Sven and I were doing in Stockholm, he booked a ticket. By the time he got there Sven was already gone, of course, well, sure, he'd already stolen my identity, what did he care?"

"Annie, why don't we just . . . ?"

"No, why don't we just *not!*" she shouts, and suddenly drops my hand, and gets to her feet, and begins pacing back and forth before the parapet. "Just leave me alone, okay? I have people telling me day and night that I should be ashamed I was even *born,* for Christ's sake, as if I have to apologize for my dual identity! Once you let them steal your identity, you know, they put you in a strait jacket," she says, and nods, and moves swiftly toward the parapet, and leans over it to look down to the street below. I reach for her and she backs away, almost losing her balance. I stand motionless, afraid to move toward her again, afraid she will throw herself over the parapet if I touch her.

"Once you've lost your identity," she says, pacing back and forth again, "they can smell the contamination all over the world, the other predators, the rapists, they come at you like a swarm of bees after honey, that's the price you pay, but nobody wants to hold your hand anymore," she says, and sighs deeply, and turns to me, her back to the parapet now, her hair blowing in the wind, across her eyes, blowing in the wind.

"There's so much traffic," she says, squinting her eyes in pain. "So much damn traffic."

"Yes, come away from there," I say.

"Not in the street, bro. *Here,*" she says, and touches her hand to her forehead. "So much traffic. It gets so *noisy,* bro."

"I know it does, honey. But we can help you. Let us help you, okay?"

"Oh help me, sure. Help! Help!" she screams in mock terror, and then giggles like a little girl. "The way Dr. *Lang* helped me, right?"

And suddenly, she sits on the parapet.

And swings her legs over the side.

I almost reach for her.

But she will jump.

Her dress riffles in the wind.

She begins mumbling, not talking to me anymore, talking instead to whatever voices she hears within. Here on the stillness of this scorching roof, the tar so hot it is bubbling in places, the traffic below muted, the voices of the city hushed and distant but rising like an invisible cloud, my sister listens to her own inner voices, and I hope to God they're not telling her to jump off this roof, I hope to God they are not.

I hold out my hand.

"Annie," I say. "Take my hand again, okay?"

"They say you're smarter than I am."

"No one's smarter than you are, honey."

"*Everybody's* fucking smarter than I am."

"Annie, honey . . . let's get off this roof, okay? Let's go someplace where we can talk."

"We are talking, bro."

"Give me your hand, hon. Let me help you . . ."

"I don't *need* help! What's *wrong* with you? Everybody thinks I need help, what the fuck is *wrong* with you people? Why do you think I need help?"

"To get off the . . . the edge of the . . . the roof there, is what I meant. To help you get down, is what I meant."

"I can get down all by myself, believe me. I can get all the way down to the street all by myself, so don't give me any *help,* okay? I know just where you're coming from. Go home, okay?"

"Not without you, Annie."

"Yes, without me. You don't want to take me home, Andy, I'm mentally ill, go ask Mama, go ask Bellevue or whoever the fuck she called, 'Are you the party with the mentally ill *relative?*' " she asks in a squeaky little nasal voice. "Jesus, the people in the health care system! Why don't they just leave me *alone?* All I want to do . . ."

She stops.

Squints.

Shakes her head.

"I don't know what I want to do anymore," she says. "I'm not even sure my work's any good anymore, do you think it's any good?"

"Yes, I think it's . . ."

"I just don't know anymore. I'm so scared it's not *good* anymore. I mean, if no one wants to buy it, how can it be any good, am I right? I thought . . . if I could find someone who *liked* my work . . . I mean, really *liked* it . . . I mean, my work is *me,* Andy, it's my soul, it's everything I *believe.* If I could find someone who appreciated it, someone who could really *love* what I do, then he could love *me,* too, don't you see? That makes sense, doesn't it? Instead of being told how worthless I am all the time? And then . . . if I could find this man . . . we could travel together—I really know a lot of beautiful places in this world, bro—we could travel *everywhere* together, oh just everywhere! I could show him all the beautiful places I've been to, I'm not stupid, you know, I really *do* know a lot about the world. I could take him everywhere, everywhere. But . . ."

She shakes her head, turns to look into my face.

"There's no one," she says.

She shakes her head again.

"I'm all alone, bro, I'm so terribly all alone," she says, "I'm so lonely all the time," and suddenly her eyes well with tears.

"Annie," I say, "you don't have to be alone."

"Don't let them put me in a strait jacket again."

"I promise."

"I'm so afraid they'll put me in a strait jacket again."

"No. No, they won't. I'll tell them not to. No one will hurt you, Annie, I promise. Let me help you. Please, honey. I want to help you."

She shakes her head.

"We're not even twins anymore, Andy. We're so different now."

"We're still twins," I say.

"I loved being your twin."

"You still are, honey."

I hold out my hand to her.

It is trembling, but it is there for her to take.

"There's too much traffic," she says.

"I don't care, Annie."

"Too much noise," she says, and shakes her head as if to clear it.

"Give me your hand, Annie. Please, dear sister, take my hand. Please. Take my hand, Annie. Please."

She opens her eyes wide. She searches my face. Suspicion crosses her eyes, and then fear again, and for just a moment, something resembling hope. She thrusts her hand out suddenly, as if against her will, as if forcing it through an invisible barrier, and I grab it at once, firmly, and pull her off the wall, and into the safety of my arms.

She is trembling with fear. Somewhere on the street below, I hear sirens approaching. She looks up into my face. Her eyes are wide and frightened. She begins trembling more violently.

"No, don't worry," I say.

Her eyes search my face.

"I'll be here," I assure her, and in that fleeting moment before she is again gone to her voices, I see in her eyes the distant glistening hope that one day she will become whole again, one day she will truly recover from that terrible moment—so very long ago—when first she lost herself so completely.

"I promise," I say.

And she nods, but does not smile, my dear sad sister, and says something I cannot comprehend as I lead her away from the edge of the roof.

About the Author

Evan Hunter is the author of twenty novels, from the 1954 bestseller and instant classic *The Blackboard Jungle* to the more recent *Candyland,* which he wrote together with Ed McBain, the pseudonym he uses on his renowned novels of the 87th Precinct. He has also written many screenplays, including the one for Alfred Hitchcock's *The Birds.*